THE TROUBLE ON JANUS

*Other books by Alfred Slote available in
Harper Trophy editions*

Clone Catcher

Hang Tough, Paul Mather

Matt Gargan's Boy

My Robot Buddy

My Trip to Alpha I

Omega Station

Rabbit Ears

The Trouble on Janus

by Alfred Slote
illustrated by James Watts

A Harper Trophy Book

Harper & Row, Publishers

Library of Congress Cataloging in Publication Data
Slote, Alfred.
  The trouble on Janus.

  Summary: Jack and his robot buddy, Danny One, set off
for the planet Janus to rescue the young King Paul from his
conniving uncle.
  [1. Robots—Fiction.   2. Science fiction]   I. Watts,
James, 1955–   , ill.   II. Title.
PZ7.S635Tt 1985   [Fic]   85-40099
ISBN 0-397-32158-9
ISBN 0-397-32159-7 (lib. bdg.)

(A Harper Trophy book)
ISBN 0-06-440216-9

Designed by Al Cetta
Published in hardcover by J. B. Lippincott, New York.
First Harper Trophy edition, 1988.

For Stanley Silverman

*Janus: An ancient Roman god usually represented
on the earliest coins with two faces.
There are also coins bearing a three-headed Janus.*

Contents

[xi]

THE TROUBLE ON JANUS

1. Beeps in the Night

It all started with beeps in the night. Three of them, to be exact:

beep beep beep

At first I thought I was dreaming those sounds. Then I heard Danny's voice. My robot buddy was talking softly, not wanting to wake me up.

"Yes, Dr. Atkins," he whispered. "I hear you, sir. Yes, sir. Jack is asleep. He can't hear me."

I opened my eyes and listened.

"But I can't do that, sir. I—yes, sir." Pause. "I'll wait outside, sir."

He clicked off his belly-button radio. I sat up. "What did Dr. Atkins want, Danny?"

Danny looked startled. "You're awake?"

"Of course I'm awake. What does he want?"

Danny sighed. "He's sending a factory air cruiser for me. He needs my help."

Gleefully I swung out of bed. "It sounds like an adventure."

"It sounds like trouble," he said.

I laughed and reached for my sneakers. For Danny, adventures are troubles. For me, troubles are adventures. Although you can't tell the difference between us, especially when I imitate a robot walk and walk stiff-in-the-knee, Dr. Atkins did program one personality difference into Danny. He made my robot buddy cautious.

"If Danny One were as reckless as you, Jack, he wouldn't be able to look after you."

Which was true. On the other hand, I looked after Danny. I'd looked after him on C.O.L.A.R. when he had disappeared into the strange underground world of runaway robots, and up at Omega Station where the evil Dr. Drago was destroying robots on his way to blowing up the world.

I'd looked after Danny in both places.

"Where did Dr. Atkins say he was going to send us this time?" I asked, getting dressed.

"He didn't say anything about 'us,' Jack. Just me."

"Hey, we're a team. He should know that by now."

Danny gave me a suspicious look. "Are you trying to get out of school in the morning?"

I laughed. I guess maybe I was. Yesterday, our teacher Miss Mortenson had given us a really hard homework assignment. We were each supposed to write a poem with rhyming words and be prepared to read our poems to the whole class.

I remembered the scene in class very well. . . .

"Poetry," Miss Mortenson had said, pursing her lips in that pruny way of hers, "is an excellent way to communicate ideas and emotions. And rhyming words is a wonderful way to help one remember things."

I couldn't have disagreed more. Who talks in rhyme? Who thinks in rhyme? Who remembers in rhyme? I couldn't rhyme words. Poetry—yuk.

I'm sure all the kids in class felt the way I did.

When I got home from school, I probably should have started working on my poem, but I didn't. I didn't say anything about it to Danny either when we went fishing in the pond behind our house.

But that night at the supper table, I guess I looked a little worried because Dad asked me if anything was wrong. I told them then about the awful homework assignment.

"I think it's a wonderful assignment," Mom said. "I only wish someone had made me write a poem when I was in sixth grade."

"Me too," said Dad. "I bet Danny can write poems." He turned to Danny. "At the time we had you programmed for sixth grade, that must have included writing poems. Did it?"

[3]

Danny grinned. I could hear his diodes whirring. He said:

> It did at the time
> And that's why I can
> Write words that will rhyme
> And lines that will scan.

Mom and Dad laughed. I didn't laugh. "What does 'scan' mean?" I asked.

"It's how you break down a line of a poem," Danny explained. "The beats and all that sort of stuff."

For the umpteenth time I wished I were a robot and not a human being. Danny gets reprogrammed every year at the Atkins Robot Factory. He gets programmed for the whole school year in ten minutes. He knows sixth grade, for instance, before it even starts. I think that's a good deal.

And then I thought: Maybe he could write my poem for me.

But I didn't say it—not out loud anyway, or in front of my folks. I knew I ought to try to do it myself first. So later that night, while Danny was giving himself a battery charge in the basement, I worked on my poem for Miss Mortenson.

I figured out a pretty good first line. About fishing.

> Has anyone seen the trout in the pond?

But then I couldn't think of a word to rhyme with "pond" except "fond." So my second line became:

A fish of which I am very fond.

That was awful. So I crossed it out and wrote and crossed out and wrote and crossed and wrote and . . . finally I put on my pajamas and tried to sleep. Sleeping solves a lot of problems.

I heard Danny come upstairs and lie down on his bed. Robots don't eat or sleep, but just as Danny sits at the table with us, so he also has a bed next to mine.

I didn't want to get into a conversation with him. I wanted to sleep. But all night long words for my fishing poem ran through my head: trout, fish, pond, hook, sinker, line, bobber. What rhymes with "trout"? with "fish"? with "pond"? with "bobber"?

Nothing. Nothing rhymes with anything. No, it doesn't. Go to sleep, Jack, you're not getting anywhere. Sleep . . . sleep . . . sleep . . .

And that was when I heard the *beep . . . beep . . . beep . . .*

Now I was all dressed and ready to go outside and wait for the factory air cruiser with Danny. But Danny wasn't ready to leave. I still hadn't answered his question, so he asked it again—grimly:

"Jack, are you trying to get out of going to school in the morning?"

I laughed again, but a little uneasily this time. He was not only my robot buddy. He was my robot conscience. "You've got smart diodes, Danny. Look, I've tried. I just can't write a poem."

"Sure you can. I'll help you."

"How are you going to help me if you're on a mission for Dr. Atkins?"

I had him there, and he knew it.

He took another tack. "Jack, your folks are going to be upset if they don't find you here in the morning."

"Hey, they'll be upset if they don't find *you*. Tell you what, let's leave them a note."

And before he could protest any more, I tore a piece of paper out of my school notebook and wrote:

> *We didn't want to wake you. Dr. Atkins called us.*
> *He needs our help again. We'll call from the factory.*
> > *Love,*
> > *Jack and*

"Now you sign too," I said.

"But it's not true, Jack. Dr. Atkins called me, not us."

"Do you want to sign it or not?"

"Maybe we ought to wake them and tell them we're leaving."

I laughed. I could read Danny's silicon chips like a video display. "You're thinking that if we woke them they wouldn't let us go. Right?"

He blushed. (He's a very expensive robot.) He nodded. "Okay. I'll sign."

He signed the note and we left it on the kitchen table. Then we tiptoed out of the house and waited outside for the Atkins factory air cruiser.

Above us, thousands and thousands of stars and planets shone in the night. As I looked at them, an ancient little poem that kids have been reciting for thousands of years came into my head.

> Twinkle twinkle little star
> How I wonder what you are

Before I could finish the poem, I heard two beeps go off inside my head, and then I heard Danny's voice inside me—I mean, he wasn't talking to me, his lips weren't moving—I heard him thinking into me:

> Up above the world so high
> Like a diamond in the sky

I stared at him. "You just finished a poem for me, didn't you?"

"Yes."

"How did you know that was what I was think-ing?"

"I'm not exactly sure but I know it's Dr. Atkins's doing. When I went in for my reprogramming last summer he told me he was going to see if he could program extrasensory perception into my microchips and try to bring a robot buddy and a human buddy even closer together."

"ESP," I said. "Danny, let's try it again. I'm thinking hard about something. You tell me what it is."

I thought about catching a trout in the pond behind our house. Last year Dad had stocked the pond with lots of fingerlings. Now those fish were big, but they were also hard to catch.

Danny closed his eyes, too. We could have been far away from each other in this experiment. I could almost feel his transistors and diodes reaching into my head. Finally, he said:

> Small went in
> Large came out
> Has a fin
> Called a

"Trout!" I shouted.

We laughed. "Do you know what this means?" I said.

"Yes," he said. "It means I'm going to see that you write a poem for Miss Mortenson. I'm going to think into you in rhyme."

"No, Danny. It means we can use ESP as a two-way communication system. We don't need radios."

I threw my arm around his shoulder. "Danny, this could be the best adventure of them all."

I looked up at the night sky full of stars and wondered what faraway diamond Dr. Atkins would send us to this time. Diamond? Yuk. I'd have to get this poetry stuff out of my head, I thought.

And Danny smiled.

2. The Kid King

Dr. Atkins was not at all pleased to see me.

"I sent for Danny One alone," he said.

"Yes, sir, but—"

"You're here. So sit down. Danny," he said, ignoring me, "I have a problem on my hands. First, let me throw Kappa System up on the ceiling."

We were in his domed laboratory at the robot factory. Dr. Atkins began throwing switches. The lights dimmed, and then up on the ceiling there appeared a three-dimensional map of the universe. Dr. Atkins flipped galaxies and planet systems until he found Kappa System.

"Here we are," he said.

A small white arrow of light darted like a fish between the stars and planets of Kappa System until it quivered to a halt next to a tiny white dot in the corner.

"That is the planet Janus," Dr. Atkins said. "A

small but wealthy planet. The form of government of Janus is a kingdom. Two years ago, the king of Janus, Paul III, died. According to my computer data, this is what the present king—Paul IV—looks like."

His computer fed a series of lines onto the three-dimensional map on the ceiling, connecting stars and planets as though a constellation was being drawn. But then Dr. Atkins pushed a button and the stars and planets faded, and all that was left were lines moving slowly.

Lines that became legs:

Then hips:

Then arms:

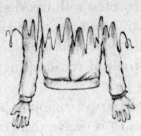

Then shoulders:

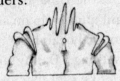

Neck:

And, finally, face:

[13]

A kid's face covered with freckles!

"That's a king?" I said, astonished. "Why he looks like he could live next door to us."

"And so he could if you lived next door to the royal palace on Janus."

Dr. Atkins picked up a computer printout. "King Paul IV," he read, "is twelve years old and is king in name only until he reaches the age of thirteen. Till then, his uncle, the Duke of Janus, is the real ruler although Paul must sit in on all meetings and decisions in the council chamber."

"You know something," Danny said a little uneasily, "I think Paul looks a lot like me and Jack."

"Yes, he does," Dr. Atkins said. "Paul weighs ninety-eight pounds and is exactly five feet tall. The same height and weight as you both."

"But we don't have all those freckles," I pointed out.

Danny nodded quickly.

"True," said Dr. Atkins. "King Paul has exactly sixteen freckles on his right cheek and twenty-one on his left."

I guess doubt must have shown on my face. Genius that he is, how could even Dr. Atkins know how many freckles a king in outer space had?

Dr. Atkins's cold blue eyes looked right through me. "There's nothing very hard about knowing that, Jack," he said. "A short time ago, I received a lasergram from the duke asking me to design and build and ship out immediately a surprise present for his nephew King Paul. The duke sent me all of Paul's dimensions—height and weight, and also his skin color and skin marks including freckles. You see, the duke wants me to build what I once built for a family named Jameson living in Metro Region VII—New Jersey—a robot buddy."

"A royal robot buddy," I said.

"Exactly. But with one important difference. The duke wants King Paul's robot buddy programmed for complete obedience."

"But that's not having a buddy," Danny said. "That's having a slave."

"Worse," said Dr. Atkins. "This robot buddy is to be programmed for complete obedience not to Paul, but to the duke."

We were silent. Around us I could hear the sounds of the factory, the hum of the assembly lines. The Atkins factory works twenty-four hours a day. As soon as Atkins robots are built and checked out, they're flown to all different parts of the universe.

"I think there's trouble on Janus," I said.

"I think so, too," said Dr. Atkins.

"What are you going to do?" Danny asked, worriedly.

"I'm going to send the duke a robot buddy for the young king. But this robot will *not* be pro-

[15]

grammed for obedience to him or anyone. It will be a clever and spunky Atkins robot who will be a detective for me and find out what's going on up there."

Danny groaned.

I clapped my hands. "What an adventure. But Danny doesn't have all the freckles Paul has."

"He could." Dr. Atkins took a jar of brown liquid off his desk.

"What's that?" I asked.

"Freckle paint."

I laughed. Danny didn't. "I don't want to go to Janus," he said.

"I'll go," I said. "Paint those freckles on me, Dr. Atkins. I can imitate a royal robot buddy perfectly." And to prove my point, I walked stiff-in-the-knee around the laboratory.

"Too risky, Jack," Dr. Atkins said. "Suppose the duke wants to look at your wiring. He'd have to cut you open to get at your computer pack. Then what?"

I didn't have an answer to that.

"No," said Dr. Atkins, taking a paintbrush with a fine tip out of a drawer, "it will have to be Danny."

"Why does it have to be either of us?" Danny said. "Tell him to buy his robot somewhere else."

"He can't," said Dr. Atkins. "Only Leopold Atkins makes robot buddies, and furthermore . . ." He looked very grave now. "Only Leopold Atkins

among robotics engineers is concerned with the possible misuse of robots. What good is engineering progress if it leads to bad ends? As a designer and builder of the greatest robots in the universe, I have a moral obligation to see that they are used to help mankind, not hurt it. Danny One, I programmed you for caution so that you could look after Jack, and you are properly cautious, but . . ." And then a gleam came into Dr. Atkins's cold blue eyes, as something occurred to him.

". . . but, well, I guess I *will* have to take a chance on Jack. Come here, Jack. I'll paint the king's freckles on you. It will be a very dangerous mission for you. You'll probably not come back alive from it."

Danny sighed. "All right, all right, paint the freckles on me. I'll go."

"I knew I could count on you, Danny," Dr. Atkins said, and dipped the brush into the freckle paint.

3. The Human Mirror

"Nineteen, twenty, twenty-one," Dr. Atkins said. He stepped back to admire his skill. "Beautiful, if I do say so myself."

He had painted sixteen freckles on Danny's right cheek and twenty-one on his left.

"I bet I don't look at all like King Paul," Danny said, hopefully.

"His very image," said Dr. Atkins.

"What do you say, Jack?" Danny turned to me.

I made a low bow. "Your Majesty," I said.

"Very funny. Well, I don't believe either of you. Do you have a mirror, Dr. Atkins?"

"I'm afraid not. There are no mirrors in robotics laboratories."

"There's one for Danny, sir," I said.

"Where?"

"Me. I could be his mirror. Just paint those freckles on me and Danny can see exactly what he looks like."

For once Dr. Atkins was impressed with me. "Jack," he said, "you're getting to be almost as smart as an Atkins robot. Hold still."

He painted sixteen freckles on my right cheek and twenty-one on my left, and when he was done Danny gave me a close examination.

"You look just like King Paul," he admitted.

"And so do you. Well, Dr. Atkins, when do we take off for Janus?"

"We? There's no 'we,' Jack. You're not going."

"If I don't go, how can Danny go? I mean, sir, you programmed him to look after me. How is he going to look after me if he's on Janus and I'm on Earth?"

I had him there, and he knew it. He frowned at me. "Jack, be reasonable. Even if I wanted to send you to Janus—which I don't—what possible excuse could there be?"

I thought fast.

"Couldn't I go as a factory sales representative? I'd go along with the royal robot buddy to make sure it arrives in good working order."

Dr. Atkins smiled. "Not bad," he said, "I do sometimes send factory representatives along with my robots. But the factory representatives are always robots themselves. Customers are impressed that Atkins robots service Atkins robots."

"I bet the duke would be even more impressed

if you sent along a human being as a factory representative. After all, it isn't every day you make a
royal robot buddy, sir. And this way you'd have two
space detectives working for you instead of one."

"Hmmm . . ." Dr. Atkins thought about it. "You
do make some good points there, Jack. Of course,
you understand, I'd have to get permission from
your family."

"Oh, they'll give it," I said. "They want Danny
and me to stick together."

And that was true.

Dr. Atkins promptly got on the Vue/Phone and
woke up our folks. (Geniuses tend to move quickly.)
Our folks hadn't read our note yet. They didn't
even know we were out of the house.

"Dr. Atkins needs us to go to the planet Janus,"
I said.

"Where's that?" Mom asked.

"Only a million miles away."

"Not in the middle of a school week, Jack," Dad said.

"You've got to write that poem for Miss Mortenson," Mom said. "You didn't do it last night."

"Danny said he'd work with me on poem writing on the trip. Won't you, Danny?"

"Yes."

"Wait a second," Dad said, peering at our faces on his Vue/Screen. "Just wait a second now. You two don't look right to me."

"I was thinking the same thing," Mom said. "Do you both have measles?"

"It couldn't be," Dad said. "We didn't program Danny for measles. Or did we, Dr. Atkins?"

The idea of anyone programming a robot for measles made us all laugh.

"No, Mr. and Mrs. Jameson," Dr. Atkins said, "what you're seeing on their faces is only a case of freshly painted freckles. Danny needs his for the mission. I'm going to take Jack's off with freckle paint remover."

"Well," Dad said, "if you really think you need them . . ."

"I do."

"Then we give our permission," Mom and Dad said, with Mom adding: "Remember to work on your poetry assignment, Jack. And both of you be careful."

[22]

I almost told her not to worry. That Danny would look after me the way he was programmed to do. But then I remembered that this time I was going along to look after him as a factory representative. I had better not tell them that or then they'd really worry.

After that, we said our goodbyes and rode up to the launching pad on the factory roof. A huge rocketship was there with letters on its side that proclaimed:

ATKINS ROBOTS: BEST IN THE UNIVERSE

In front of the landing ramp leading to the air locks was a box about six feet long. A red shipping label was attached to it.

From: Atkins Robot Factory, Earth
To: Duke of Janus, Janus
Contents: One Royal Robot Buddy

THIS SIDE UP THIS SIDE UP THIS SIDE UP THIS SIDE

"Do I have to travel in that?" Danny asked.

"It's just a regular factory shipping crate," Dr. Atkins said.

"It looks like a coffin."

"Nonsense. I deliver robots to all parts of the universe in crates exactly like that. In fact, I want that crate back after you're delivered. However, if it makes you feel better, Danny, you don't have to get nailed into it till just before you land on Janus. Here's our chief pilot Fred One. Fred, you remember Jack and Danny?"

Fred One was a big, friendly-faced robot with wide mustaches.

"I do, sir. But they look a bit different to me."

"We've got freckles now, Fred," I said.

"Well, so you do. I've always wanted a few freckles myself."

"Bring these two space detectives back safely, Fred, and I'll give you a hundred freckles on each cheek."

Fred laughed. "And where am I to take them this time, sir?"

"Janus."

"Janus? That's a nice sleepy little planet. Good landing pad at Janus City Spaceport. Hardly ever busy. Should be an easy trip. Which of them goes into the crate, sir?"

"Danny does." Dr. Atkins put his hands on Danny's shoulders. "Danny One," he said gravely, "I want you to remember at all times that you are an Atkins robot—intelligent, brave, and spunky."

"I'm not spunky," Danny said.

"You're spunkier than you think. Don't forget that you're supposed to have been programmed for complete obedience to the duke. You must do what he tells you to do until you find out what he's up to."

"And then what, sir?"

"Then you and Jack contact Fred, who'll have a reason to keep the rocketship on Janus, and return with him."

"We'll have a sudden case of engine trouble," Fred said, with a wink.

"As for you, Jack," Dr. Atkins said, turning to me. "Don't let the duke pay you for the robot right away. Tell him the warranty is only good if you're there to service the robot for a while. Is that clear?"

"Yes, sir."

"Then goodbye to you both, and good luck."

We shook hands. Then Fred One picked up the shipping crate and we followed him up the ramp, into the ship. I couldn't help thinking it was a little like following the coffin in a funeral procession.

We were between the outer air lock and the inner air lock when Danny grabbed my arm. "The freckle paint remover, Jack. He didn't take off your freckles, and we don't have any."

"You're right."

"No problem," Fred said. "I'll get him on the radio."

Which is what he did. He pushed a button and radioed Dr. Atkins, who was going to watch our blastoff from the roof tower.

"Jack has his freckles on and we don't have any freckle paint remover, sir," Fred radioed.

Silence.

"I don't make many mistakes," Dr. Atkins said, "but I did just now. I'll have it brought to you immediately."

Danny and I went back and opened the air locks. Seconds later a robot technician came up the ramp with a jar of freckle paint remover. It was a thick, whitish-looking liquid.

"It's powerful stuff," the technician warned me, "so just use it where the freckles are."

"I'll apply it to him myself," Danny said. He put the jar on the flight console.

The technician left. We closed the air locks and Fred received permission from Dr. Atkins to blast off.

Up came the ramp, and the rocket motors burst into noise. The landing legs retracted and slowly we rose from the roof of the Atkins Robot Factory. We could see Dr. Atkins in the tower watching us.

The tower got smaller and smaller until he was only a white dot inside it, then the factory got smaller and smaller and then the city around the factory and then the country around the city around the factory around the tower and then the whole planet got small and round and blue and white until with a bang, crash, shudder—we hit Earth's gravity curtain.

And Earth, behind us, disappeared.

4. A Bump in Space

Within the Earth system there's always a lot of traffic: space colony shuttles, heavy-duty space trucks carrying workers and raw materials back and forth between moon and Earth and between the moon and the space colonies. And, of course, there's always a lot of old junk orbiting in space—old satellites, space stations, work stations, obsolete weapons systems.

On the other side of the gravity curtain, Fred One concentrated on maneuvering our ship between shuttles and trucks and space taxis and debris, complaining about how crowded outer space was becoming, until we were past most of the Earth system traffic, past the moon, and then Fred relaxed and set a computer course for Kappa System and the planet Janus.

"We'll be there by late afternoon," he announced.

"Let's get started on the homework, Jack," Danny said.

"Do we have to?"

"Yes. It's time for you to work on a poem."

"What about?"

"Poems can be about anything."

"You do one first, Danny."

"Jack, you're stalling."

"No. Honest. I want to see what you come up with. Make up a poem about our mission to Janus. What you think will happen."

Danny looked at me and then shook his head. "Pick another subject."

I grinned. "You said you could write a poem about anything."

"All right," Danny said. "Let me work on it . . ."

I could hear his diodes humming. His computer was working stuff out. "Okay," he said. "You ready?"

"Shoot."

Grim faced, Danny recited:

> A robot named Danny
> And a young lad named Jack
> Went off to Janus
> And never came back.

I laughed. "That's a terrible poem."

"What's terrible about it?"

"It's not true. We'll come back."

"Poems aren't true or false, Jack. And besides, that's how I feel about this mission. Anyway, the important part for your homework is how the poem works. *Jack* rhymes with *back*. It's an ABCB rhyme scheme, each line has six syllables and you can hear the rhythm, can't you: da-dum, da-dum, da-dum, da-dum—"

"Are you all right, Danny?" Fred called from the flight console.

"No, he's not," I said. "His computer just broke. He keeps saying da-dum, da-dum, da-dum, da-dum."

"Thanks a lot, Jack," Danny said.

I laughed. "You asked for it with all those da-dums."

"Your turn now. You start a poem and we'll work on it together."

"I'm sleepy. I've been awake since the middle of the night. I'm going to take a little nap on the deck."

I lay down on the floor of the ship, next to the

factory crate. Danny looked unhappy with me. He knew I was getting out of homework, and I guess he was trying to figure out ways for me to work on poetry.

I closed my eyes. "Wake me up if anything interesting happens out there."

The odds were against anything interesting happening in outer space. Outer space is a boring place. That's a rhyme. Maybe I could write a poem, if I didn't have better, more exciting things to do. Like sleeping.

I fell asleep. When I woke up, I could hear Fred and Danny talking quietly in the front of the ship. I lay there with my eyes closed as our ship hurtled through dark space and listened to them. Danny was asking about all the unusual planets Fred had been to while piloting rocketships for Dr. Atkins.

"Well," Fred said softly, "the planet Diaperus was a pretty unusual place. Very noisy."

"How come?" Danny asked.

"Full of babies. It's the planetary day care center for the whole Upsilon system."

"What kind of robots did you deliver there?" Danny asked.

"Atkins nursemaid robots."

"What's the quietest planet you delivered to?" I asked, joining them at the console.

"Canus," Fred said.

"Are you ready to work on a poem now, Jack?" Danny asked.

"No. Why is Canus quiet?"

"It's full of old people on canes who sit and doze a lot," Fred said.

"What kind of robots did you deliver there?"

"Nursemaid robots," Fred said. "And then there are planets I've heard of but never been to that are really supposed to be strange . . ."

And as we rolled through space, Fred told yarns about planets where fishes ruled because there was no land, and a planet so far from its warming star that people lived under the ice in neonlike tubes and were long and thin and squirted from one place to another in their tubes. Fred had heard of a planet where pigs talked and owls drew pictures, a planet of people with two heads who were always talking to themselves. There was a planet where trees danced and rocks sang and rivers ran up and down vertically and volcanic mountains spoke to each other in puffs of smoke. And there were planets, Fred said, like Earth, only a thousand years behind, where people still fought wars.

"It's a big universe out there," Fred said, "it just rolls on and on. Dr. Atkins says there's at least a billion other Dr. Atkinses out there with his exact name and brain making and selling Atkins Robots. He says everything repeats itself in space. Well, that may be so, but wherever I've been I've never met another Dr. Leopold Atkins. One of him is enough for me to handle. Hullo. What's that?"

A space station came into view off to the left. A small one. An outstation. Fred checked his instruments. "You two got me talking so much I didn't realize we were in Kappa System already," he said.

More satellite stations came into view. Some had people on board who waved to us. Others were automated. We could see the navigational lights of space cruisers crisscrossing our flight pattern, and we could hear pilots talking to each other over their radios, discussing navigational hazards around Janus.

"We should be getting landing coordinates from the Janus City Spaceport," Fred said.

He pushed in his directional signaler, which let ground stations know that a rocketship from outer space was approaching their space control system.

Sure enough, seconds later our radio burst into sound.

"Janus City Spaceport to Atkins rocketship," a voice crackled. "Janus City Spaceport to Atkins rocketship," the crackling voice repeated. It sounded excited. Not like your usual unemotional spaceport control officer's voice.

Fred pushed in the "send" button. "Atkins rocketship," he said.

"I scope you. Due to heavy traffic here your landing area has been changed to an auxiliary field at midnight. Here are your new coordinates."

And then the voice read off a series of numbers, changing one, correcting another (the voice sounded nervous), that Fred entered into his computer. The voice signed off abruptly.

"That's odd," Fred said. "Janus is the quietest planet in Kappa System, and suddenly it's so busy we have to land at an auxiliary field at midnight."

"Maybe it's just an excuse to keep our arrival a secret," I said. "After all, the royal robot buddy is supposed to be a surprise present."

"Good point," Fred said. "And with our sign advertising Atkins Robots on the side of the ship, it would be a dead giveaway. Well, at least we won't have to orbit too much. Janus is a small planet, and time goes by quickly there. Though I don't like circling any planet too long. You never know what people put up in orbit these days."

Besides satellite stations, Janus seemed to put a lot of trash in orbit—old boxes, bathtubs, tools, appliances, solar car parts. Fred explained to us that there was limited space on Janus and so they liked to dump things in outer space.

"Some of the stuff falls back onto Janus, some stays in orbit, some drifts off and flows on through the universe. Whoops!"

Our ship bounced off something.

"Air pocket," Fred explained. "Pockets of air are always escaping from Janus's thin gravity. It's awkward for pilots but a good thing for any human who may have the bad luck to fall out of a spaceship."

Since I was the only human in our spaceship, I looked out a window to see if I could spot the air pocket. But air's hard to see unless something's inside it, breathing it.

The computer sounded a warning.

"Time to go down," Fred said. "Hang on now."

He put the ship into a steep dive. And then, with a quick bang and a shudder, we were through the thin Janus gravity curtain and into that planet's atmosphere.

It was a pretty bumpy atmosphere, too. Much bumpier than Earth's. Fred complained about it, saying they ought to clean it up a bit. He held on tightly to the steering controls, and then, when we seemed to have hit some smooth air, he said: "All right, time for Danny to climb into the crate. We'll be on the ground in less than two minutes."

We could see the lights of Janus below.

"Better get in," I said to Danny.

He looked glumly at the crate. "I get bad vibrations from it."

I laughed. "Those bad vibrations are from the bumps in the atmosphere. Don't worry. I'll stick close to you."

Danny climbed into the crate, lay down on his back, looked up at me, and said: "Oh no."

"Now what's the matter?"

"We forgot to take the freckles off your face."

He climbed out of the crate. "Give me your handkerchief, Jack," he said. He took the jar of freckle paint remover off the console and removed the lid. Then he dipped one end of my hanky into the thickish stuff and was going to dab off a few freckles when the ship hit a really big bump of Janus air. We all jumped. Including the freckle paint remover. The thick white stuff flew up into Danny's face. He looked startled. I laughed, and then I stopped laughing and stared at him.

"What's the matter?" he asked.

"Your freckles. They're gone."

"Oh no."

"Oh yes."

"It's not funny, Jack. We don't have any more freckle paint. Fred, we've got to turn around and go back to Earth."

"Too late," Fred said. "We're down. And someone's out there waiting for us. Looks like a big official. Got a big car with a laser cannon mounted on top."

There could be no going back now, I thought. I knew what I had to do, and I did it: I climbed into the crate.

"No, Jack!" Danny said.

"Nail the lid shut."

"I won't let you. It's too dangerous. Suppose the duke or Paul want to examine your wiring. Dr. Atkins said they might."

"Don't let them. You're the factory representative now. Remember what Dr. Atkins said: Atkins robots service Atkins robots. That's the way it usually is." I grinned at him. "Now you can really look after me."

"Ramp's down," Fred announced, "and here comes our official greeter. I'm going to open the air locks."

"Quick, Danny. Nail it shut."

Danny had no choice. Although it ran against every silicon chip in his computer, he had to do it. He slid the lid over the crate and nailed it shut. The vibrations from each blow of the hammer went painfully through my body.

When the lid was nailed shut, Danny pressed his mouth against the box and said: "I'll hammer some air holes for you to breathe, Jack."

He did. And they hurt, too.

5. Jack in the Box

I don't know if you've ever been nailed inside a box, but I can tell you it's no picnic. In fact, it's a panic.

My heart began to pound. I told myself to calm down, that if I panicked I'd breathe even harder and use up my tiny air supply.

Think about other things, I told myself, happy things—an open sky, climbing an apple tree, swimming in the pond. Don't think about being nailed into a dark box.

So I thought about sun and blue sky and a pond and an apple tree in blossom and slowly my heart stopped pounding. And I calmed down. Then I started thinking that all would be well because even though I was pretending to be an Atkins robot, the robot I was pretending to be was a present to the king of Janus. And Paul would look after me. Kids always took care of expensive presents. Danny had been an expensive present to me. And I'd taken good care of him—or had I? Here we were in trouble a million miles from home and all because I couldn't keep my nose out of adventures. Danny hadn't wanted to leave home at all. I had to talk him into it. I sure had taken good care of both of us, hadn't I?

That kind of thinking got my heart pounding all over again, so hard I thought I was making vibrations on the deck of the ship. Then I realized the vibrations were coming from outside the crate. Someone with heavy boots was walking up to it.

I held my breath. I heard a squeak. A mouse? It couldn't be. Then there was another squeak, and now a thin slice of light appeared above my nose. The squeaks were the sounds of nails being pried up.

I heard Danny's voice.

"You'll notice, Mr. Duke, that Dr. Atkins has programmed the royal robot buddy to breathe like a human being. Of course, it really isn't breathing."

Clever Danny. He was doing two things at once. Letting me know the duke himself was present and explaining my breathing to the duke.

"Excellent," said a new voice, "now open the crate all the way, please."

It was a voice used to exercising authority.

"You'll notice, too, sir, that this Atkins robot can

[40]

do everything a human being can except walk smoothly."

Danny was reminding me not to forget my robot walk.

"I understand. Now open the crate. I am anxious to see the royal robot buddy."

But Danny went on talking.

"This robot has a computer pack for a brain. That pack must never be tampered with."

Thanks, Danny.

"Mr. Factory Representative, I make it a practice never to argue with robots, even when they represent the Atkins factory. Time is growing short. A Janus night is a good deal shorter than an Earth night. Either you open that lid right now or I will borrow your hammer and do it myself."

"I'll do it, sir," Danny said quickly.

And one by one he pried up the rest of the nails and slid back the lid. Light flooded my eyes. At first everything was fuzzy, but then a man's face swam into focus. A cold thin face with bluish-gray eyes that revealed nothing.

The Duke of Janus regarded me silently, and then a thin smile played on his lips.

"Dr. Atkins's reputation is not unfounded. The robot is Paul's exact likeness."

He peeled off a white glove and leaned toward me.

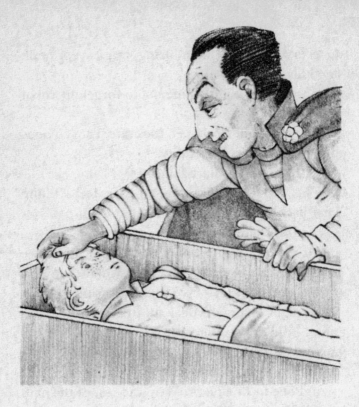

"It breathes like a human being. And its meta-plastic skin . . ."

He touched my forehead with an icicle-cold hand.

". . . is just like human flesh."

I shuddered.

His smile widened. "And it reacts like a human being, too. Wonderful."

He turned back to Danny and took an envelope out of his pocket.

"Here is Dr. Atkins's money. You will return to

Earth, Mr. Factory Representative, and tell the great man that the Duke of Janus congratulates him on this royal robot buddy. It's just what I ordered."

"I'll be glad to do that, sir," Danny replied, "but my orders from Dr. Atkins are to accompany this robot to the king's palace in order to make sure it is in good working condition when presented to the king."

"Not necessary," the duke said pleasantly, "I can assure you the king will be extremely pleased with his present." He turned to me again. "Robot," he said, "I am the Duke of Janus. I command you to rise from that crate."

An idea came to me. I lay perfectly still.

"I said—rise from that crate!"

I didn't move a muscle.

Danny caught on. "You see, sir, the trip must have jarred something loose. I'll take him to the palace and examine him there."

The duke held out a hand toward Danny. "The hammer, please."

"What for?" Danny asked.

"It has been my experience that what has been jarred loose can often be jarred tight again."

And then he took the hammer out of Danny's paralyzed hand and stepped toward me.

"If you hit him," Danny said desperately, "the warranty is no longer valid."

"I'll take that risk," the duke said. "Just one hard tap on the side of its head might do the trick." He raised the hammer.

I sat up.

The duke laughed. "A very intelligent robot. It doesn't like to be struck. Can you talk, robot?"

"Yes, sir. Where am I, sir?"

"You are on the planet Janus. And I am the Duke of Janus. Does that name mean anything to you?"

"Yes, Master."

A look of pleasure crossed his cruel face. "Good. Now I command you to rise from the crate, pick it up, and carry it to the solar car at the foot of the landing ramp."

It was an order I didn't want to carry out. But I had to. I rose stiffly—I wasn't faking that—and picked up the crate. It wasn't that heavy but it was awkward. A robot would have had an easier time with it than I did.

"Stop!" the duke commanded.

I stopped. He ripped off the red shipping label. "It wouldn't be much of a surprise for the king if he saw this tag, would it? And that, young factory representative, is why your ship must leave Janus immediately. The Atkins sign on the side of the ship could be seen by everyone. Royal robot buddy, why are you standing there? You heard my orders. Go to the solar car."

I looked helplessly at Danny and Fred as I staggered past them with the crate on my shoulder.

I went out through the inner and outer air locks and down the ramp. It wasn't easy walking downward stiff-in-the-knee and carrying a crate, too. But I had to. The duke was coming right behind me.

About twenty feet from the bottom of the ramp was a long, sleek solar car. On its top was mounted a laser cannon. The kind only the military have back home. It looked frightening. It was pointed toward our rocketship.

"Put the crate in the back," the duke said.

I did that.

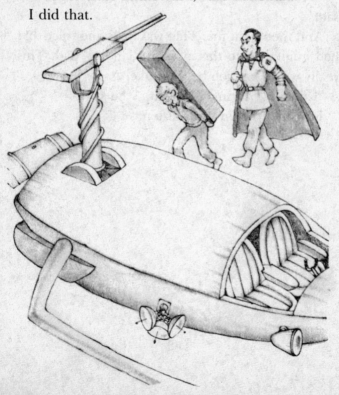

"Now climb back into the crate," he said.

I did that too.

"Now pull the lid over you."

I did that too. But he didn't nail it shut. He had no hammer.

I heard him go around and get in front. It bothered me that someone as important as the Duke of Janus was doing all this alone, but then I guess it really was important to him to have the royal robot buddy be a complete surprise to King Paul.

I heard the car radio transmitter click on.

"The Duke of Janus to Atkins rocketship," he said.

And then it hit me. That was the same voice that had guided us to this auxiliary landing pad. This really was a solo job by the duke.

"Come in, Atkins rocketship," he said.

I pushed the lid up to listen.

6. "Call Me Uncle"

"We're right here, sir," Fred's voice came crackling back over the radio.

"I see that. Why haven't you blasted off yet?"

"We seem to have a malfunction in one of our motors, sir. I'll need time to repair it."

"There is no time, robot pilot. Besides, you don't need all your motors to leave Janus. We're a small planet with a weak gravity pull. You can leave on one motor and you will."

"Impossible, sir."

"Then I'm afraid I must destroy your ship. The package you delivered must be a complete surprise. I do not want an Atkins Factory rocketship here on Janus. If you're not gone in thirty seconds, I will fire the laser cannon at your ship. And your ship, I assure you, will not last long."

Now there were no sounds on the radio. I could imagine Fred and Danny trying to decide what to do next.

"You now have twenty seconds," the duke said.

He would, I thought, blow them up. It was his planet.

Fred's voice came over the radio. "I will be able to leave with the ship, sir, but the factory representative wishes to check out the royal robot buddy. He's programmed to do that, sir. He's a robot himself, you see, and —"

"Tell the factory representative to deprogram himself. The royal robot buddy works perfectly. You now have fifteen seconds."

Silence.

Now Danny got on the radio. "Dr. Atkins has ordered me to accompany the royal robot buddy."

"Dr. Atkins's orders have no authority on Janus. You now have ten seconds. I am arming the cannon."

The duke punched a button on the car console.

"Eight," he said. "Seven, six, five, four—"

There was a tremendous explosion, a roar of rocket engines. On the roof of the car I saw a reflection of flames from engine exhausts. And then I saw a great rising of smoke, and through the smoke, the Atkins rocketship rose . . .

. . . and my heart sank.

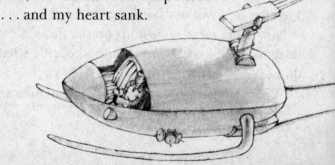

I would have cried if I was certain the royal robot buddy had been programmed for tears.

The solar car rose in the air and I felt us gliding. How long we traveled I wasn't sure. I felt turns but no bumps. Perhaps we traveled for twenty minutes. I felt the car slowly come to a stop and then sink a few feet and touch ground.

"Who goes there?" a voice called out in the night.

"The Duke of Janus," said the voice from the front of the car.

"Sorry, Your Grace," said the guard. "I didn't recognize you. Pass on through."

Now the solar car bumped its way over what felt like cobblestones. And every bump went through me. Finally we stopped again. The car engine was turned off. More voices outside. Someone giving orders. "Attention. Squad forward." Soldiers.

"No need for all that," the duke said. "I have a heavy package, Sergeant. I'll need two men to carry it up to the council chamber."

"Yes, sir."

More orders outside.

I heard the duke's voice, now close to the lid, saying softly: "Don't say a word to anyone, robot. Do you understand?"

"Yes, Master."

"Shsh." He pushed the lid down as tightly as he could.

"Sergeant, this is a very fragile vase in here. I want it handled with care."

"Yes, Your Grace. You heard the duke, men. Be careful."

I felt myself lifted up and carried carefully out of the car. I felt the night air seep inside the crate, and then I could tell we were inside a building.

"Gently, gently," urged the duke.

Next I knew we were in an elevator because I felt my stomach go swoosh as we rose rapidly and swoosh again as we came to a quick stop.

Now we were moving again. I heard doors open, close. Finally I heard the duke saying, "Gently. Set it down very gently."

Down went the crate and me, too.

"Excellent," said the duke. "Thank you, Sergeant."

"Attention," barked the sergeant, and I heard the sounds of retreating boots. And then silence. A door closed. More silence. The duke was cautious.

Then I heard him come up to the crate, kneel down. He slid the lid off and looked down at me, that same thin smile on his lips.

"That wasn't such a bad trip, was it, robot?"

"No, Master."

"You may rise now and look around. You are now inside the royal council chamber of the king's palace on Janus."

I climbed out of the crate and looked about. The first thing that met my eye was a huge domed ceiling, clear glass, and through it the night sky of Janus twinkled down at me. The dome was framed with gold and silver ornaments.

The next thing I noticed were the walls of the room. They were adorned with portraits of what looked like past kings of Janus. Each one wore a six-pointed gold crown on his head.

Next I noticed the side of the room. It was huge. There were benches and chairs along the side. A door leading to a closet or another room. And then at the far end of the room, away from the main entrance, at the end of a long purple carpet, there was a throne.

A heavy golden throne.

But there was something odd about it. And it took me a moment to realize what it was.

The throne was on wheels! The golden throne was really a golden wheelchair. I stared at it.

The duke watched me, amused. "Well, robot, what do you think of it?"

I didn't know what to say, so I said nothing.

"This is the royal council chamber," the duke said. "It's here that the king sits each day while I give audiences to his subjects. The king will give audiences and make decisions when . . ." He paused, interrupting himself, and looked at me closely in the better light of the council chamber. In the rocketship he couldn't study my features too closely, but here he could . . . and did. I saw him particularly examine the freckles on each cheek. He nodded approvingly and permitted himself a smile as he finished his line of thought:

". . . or *if* he reaches thirteen."

I would not understand the meaning of that till later.

"Robot," he snapped, and now his voice changed; it was filled with power and command.

"Yes, Master."

"Go and sit on the throne."

"Yes, Master."

I walked stiff-in-the-knee over the purple carpet and sat down on the golden wheelchair throne. The duke walked over to a large cabinet on the side, pulled out a drawer, and from the drawer took a six-pointed gold crown. The same gold crown that sat on the heads of the previous kings of Janus in the pictures.

"The final test," he murmured.

He came back to me and placed the crown on my head. Then he stepped back and studied me once more. Finally, he bowed his head.

"Your Majesty," he said.

My heart skipped a beat.

"Master," I asked, "who am I?"

His bluish-gray eyes glittered. His face was amused and cruel at the same time. He was truly a two-faced man.

"From now on you are the king of Janus—Paul IV. Do you understand that?"

I nodded. "Yes, Master."

"And from now on, dear Nephew, you must call me uncle. Say 'uncle.' "

"Uncle."

"Beautiful. It's music to my ears. Now, dear Nephew, although you are officially the king, you will, of course, continue to obey me as you are programmed to do. However, and this is important, no one but no one is to find out that you are a robot. Is that clear?"

"Yes, Mast—Uncle."

"You are King Paul, confined to a wheelchair because you have contracted a crippling muscle disease that leaves you unable to walk and barely able to talk. Is that clear?"

"Yes, Uncle."

It was all becoming very clear. The only thing that would give me away as a robot would be my walk. And most likely my voice wasn't the same timbre as Paul's, so from now on I was to talk in a whisper. A great disease. The duke had worked it out in detail—almost, I thought.

"Uncle, what will people say when I don't grow?"

Or what will you say when I do?

"People will say nothing, dear Nephew. Your disease is one that will prevent you from growing physically as well as mentally. You see, Nephew, you will be twelve years old the rest of your life. A royal doctor will certify you as unable to ever rule in your own name."

And there it finally was. His plan. He would rule Janus forever in the name of King Paul IV, who would never reach manhood or kinghood.

"And now, dear Nephew, it is getting late. And while you don't need sleep, I do. So quickly, I will tell you what your first days on the throne will be like.

"To begin with, you may as well stay right where you are for the night. The less moving around you do, the safer it is. No one will bother you during the night. I'm going to lock the door with a special key. It's better to be safe than sorry.

"The morning council begins just after dawn. You need do absolutely nothing. Just sit on your throne and stare ahead of you. That," he said, with that same thin cruel smile, "will be perfect royal behavior.

"Very early in the session breakfast will be brought to you. This is a tradition. It gave Paul something to do—eat."

"What will I do, Uncle?"

"You will do nothing. The maid has orders to move it quickly into your bedroom. After a while I will come in and dispose of it myself. And by next week I will also dispose of this stupid tradition.

"The afternoon session will be a repeat of the morning. You will continue to sit in your chair and stare at nothing. Do you have that, Nephew?"

"Yes, Uncle."

"However, on the day after tomorrow there will be a great event in your honor. The whole kingdom is being urged to come to the royal square to see you on the balcony."

"What will I do then, Uncle?"

"Why nothing, of course. You will sit and stare at them. And now, Nephew, I'm going to tuck you in for the night."

By tuck he meant lock. Key in hand he went to the door.

"Uncle," I said.

"Yes, Nephew."

"What happened to the real King Paul?"

It was a dangerous question to have asked. A look of anger came over his face, and then disappeared as quickly. "Why, Nephew, the real Paul is sitting on his wheelchair throne in the royal council chamber. Goodnight, Nephew." He closed and locked the door.

"Good night, Uncle," I said, quietly.

The royal palace was a royal prison.

7. King for a Day

While a throne's a swell place to see the world and let the world see you, it's a tough spot to sleep.

I got off the throne and lay down on the purple carpet. But tired as I was, I couldn't sleep there either. I was too excited. Worries about Danny and Fred raced through my brain. Were they orbiting Janus right now? Getting ready to sneak back down? How would they get past the soldiers guarding the palace? Could they help me find Paul? Or where his body was buried?

Those thoughts kept me awake. But the thought that got me up off the carpet and back on the throne again was this: Janus is a small planet. Its nights are short. Suppose the duke came in at the crack of dawn and found me asleep on the carpet?

So I got back on the throne and dozed on and off, waking everytime a floorboard in the castle creaked, or a door opened, or a clock struck.

Once I dreamed something struck me on the

arm. I woke up. My crown had fallen off and was lying across my wrist. I put it back on my head and was then aware that something had changed in the room.

There was sunlight coming into it. Rays of sun were coming down through the great glass dome in the ceiling.

What a piece of luck that the crown had fallen off and woke me up. I sat up straight. Sure enough, I soon heard footsteps in the hall. Then I heard a key turning in the lock. The door opened. The duke entered the room and closed, but did not lock, the door behind him.

"Well, Nephew, did you—" He caught himself and laughed, a short humorless laugh. "I was going to ask you if you slept well, but that would have been a foolish question. Now, in exactly fifteen seconds your day will officially begin. Remember—say nothing. Stare straight ahead."

"Yes, Uncle."

The duke went over to a button on the wall and pushed it. I heard a bell ring in the hall outside, and then there were the sounds of trumpets and drums out there. The door swung open and a tall, gray-haired soldier entered the room. He carried a big sword in front of him. He saluted me with it and then did an about-face and thumped the point of the sword down onto the floor and cried out:

[59]

"Hear ye! The king is on his throne. Let this Janus day officially begin!"

And with that a stream of people rushed into the council chamber—old people and young, rich and poor, soldiers and civilians—carrying petitions, calling out grievances, quarreling, shouting. There was lots of noise.

The duke clapped his hands. Instantly there was silence.

"King Paul is back on his throne but, as you can plainly see, he's not well. So, please, a little order in the council chamber."

The tall soldier with the sword bowed.

"We just want to say how sorry we are about his majesty's illness, Your Grace, and how glad we are to see him again."

"That's fine, Sergeant," the duke replied. "On behalf of King Paul who cannot walk or talk above a whisper, I give you thanks. Tomorrow at noon the king will present himself to all the public. But today we have business to—"

The duke stopped as a girl my age in a blue and white apron elbowed her way through the crowd carrying a tray of food over her head.

"Make way for the king's breakfast," the sergeant cried out. "Make way for the king's breakfast!"

The duke frowned, but there was nothing he could do about this "tradition"—yet.

Partly because I was hungry and partly because I'd never seen anything like it, I stared hard at the food on her tray. Every planet has its own cuisine but Janus outdid them all. There were square bananas and octagonal apples, a flask of multi-striped juice and three hotcakes that looked like ice cream cones. (I *think* they were hotcakes.)

The girl curtsied to me, but there was a mischievous look in her dark eyes and a hint of a mocking smile on her lips.

"We hope your appetite is good this morning, Your Majesty," she said.

"Put the tray in the king's bedroom, Tina," the duke snapped. "He will eat later. We have much work to do here now, and because of his illness he's not very hungry."

But I am very hungry, I thought. I haven't had anything to eat since dinner on earth more than twenty-four hours ago.

"Begin the business of the state," the duke called out, and gave me a quick look that meant, I knew, to start staring lifelessly ahead of me.

Which I did, though pangs of hunger beat a rhythm inside my stomach.

The morning went on and on and on. I was hungry and the people were boring. All they did was read long petitions to the duke.

Two neighbors were having a fight about a tree

that bordered on their land. Onto one property the tree dropped Janus apples; onto the other property it dropped Janus worms. The man who got worms wanted to cut down the tree. (He was no fisherman, I guess.) The man who got the apples wanted the tree left alone.

"In the name of King Paul," the duke announced, "I order you who receive the apples to share those apples and you who receive the worms to share those worms. Further, I order that the

money from every third apple sold should be paid
to the king."

I could see why the duke wanted to rule.

Next there was an argument between a busi-
nessman and a businesswoman about who owed
who money. The duke settled the matter by having
them both pay the "king." There were disputes between towns, taxes to be collected, debts to be paid,
marriages, divorces, births to be registered and fees
for everything paid to the "king." There were solar

car accidents and fines to be paid to the "king" by the guilty parties. There were treaties to be signed with space colonies with lawyers' fees paid to the "king." There were budgets to be worked out, and on and on it went with no end of people coming in to have their problems settled by the duke, who collected from each of them in the name of the "king."

Finally, it was time for lunch. The tall sergeant of the guard ordered all the petitioners out. The duke wheeled me past a line of soldiers with laser rifles drawn at attention. He wheeled me into a small room. A bedroom. There was only a bed and a table in there and a door leading somewhere. On the table was the breakfast tray that the girl named Tina had brought in earlier. My mouth watered at the sight of the fruit and cakes, strange as they appeared.

The duke wheeled me against a far wall. "You will sit here, Nephew, until I fetch you for the afternoon session."

"Uncle, shouldn't I pretend to eat some of the food? We don't want to make people suspicious."

"You can't pretend to eat, Nephew. Pieces of apple and banana would fall into your wires. However, your point is well taken. Some of that food *must* be eaten right now."

Whereupon he proceeded to eat my breakfast.

He ate the octagonal apple and the square banana and drank half of my striped juice and was starting on the hotcakes when I said:

"Uncle, don't you think you better leave a little bit behind? I'm supposed to be sick. Sick kings don't eat a lot of food."

He stared at me. "Atkins is a genius. You're absolutely right, Nephew. I'll leave the hotcakes. And I should be back in a little while. I have a luncheon meeting of the Ministers of Trade."

The pig! Stuffing himself while I was starving.

I waited till I was sure he was out of the council chamber. Then I jumped out of the wheelchair and attacked the hotcakes. I had half a hotcake in my mouth and the other half in my hand when there was a sharp knock on my door.

I swallowed what I had in my mouth, and put the other half in my pocket, and got back into my wheelchair throne.

"Who's there?" I said, forgetting I wasn't to speak to anyone.

There was a silence as though the person I was talking to also realized I who could not talk just had.

And then a girl's voice said: "It's me, Tina, Your Majesty. I've come to collect your breakfast tray."

But when she spoke there didn't seem any surprise in her voice.

"I'm not finished eating."

To my amazement she laughed, and then, without asking permission, she entered the room.

She grinned at me and didn't curtsy either.

"And how is Your Majesty today?" she said, and examined the tray with the apple core, the banana peel, and the two remaining hotcakes.

She frowned at that. "Did your majesty eat up or throw the food in the toilet?"

I stared at her. She was really cheeky.

Nor did she wait for an answer. She opened the other door in the room and looked in there. "The toilet's clean," she said. She closed the door and came back to me. "You've done something else with that food, haven't you, Your Majesty?"

There was more than impudence in her tone. There was mockery, too.

"Just who do you think you're talking to?" I said angrily. (I guess wearing a crown can go to your head.)

"You, *Your Majesty*," she said, underlining those last two words with a heavy edge of sarcasm. She slipped the two remaining hotcakes into the pocket of her apron.

"Wait a second. What do you think you're doing with those hotcakes?"

"There's someone who needs them more than you, *Your Majesty*."

Again she underlined those last two words as though she didn't believe them for a second. My heart skipped a beat. A sudden fear grabbed at me.

Tina paused at the door, the tray in hand.

She grinned. "I left the flask, *Your Majesty,* in case you get thirsty, too."

And left.

She knew! But how? And what would she do with her knowledge?

At that moment I was so worried I almost forgot I was starving to death and still had half a hotcake in my pocket and a flask of striped juice on the table.

Calm down, Jack Jameson. Fear is exhausting. Get some food into you. You need energy.

I ate the hotcake and drank the juice and thought. I had to find out exactly how much Tina knew.

But there was no time for it now. Already the afternoon session was starting. Out in the council chamber I could hear the duke greeting people. And then his footsteps coming to the door.

He entered and closed the door behind him.

"Well, Nephew," he asked softly, "are you ready for the afternoon session?"

"Yes, Uncle," I whispered.

"Good. Remember, be silent and stare out."

I debated whether I should tell him I'd already

spoken—to Tina—and decided not to. I didn't want to get him angry at me.

"Yes, Uncle," I whispered.

He opened the door and wheeled me back into the huge room, and there I sat all afternoon while more petitions and grievances were read and argued. I was still hungry and still bored, and now also worried about Tina and what she knew.

If this was what it was like to be a king, it was a terrible job. But how did one get out of it?

8.   Brief Escape

Fortunately, Janus days are as short as Janus nights. When the sun went down, the tall, gray-headed sergeant of the guard declared the business day over. Once again I was wheeled out by the duke, who announced to everyone that he would feed me personally.

"Isn't it wonderful how he looks after the king," I heard someone murmur.

The duke smiled tenderly as he wheeled me out. A more two-faced person I'd never met. My only consolation was that I was more two-faced than he. I was even three-faced. I was a boy pretending to be a robot pretending to be a boy.

"Well, Nephew, how did you like your first day on the throne?" he asked me, once the door was closed behind us.

"It was very boring," I said bluntly.

That startled him. And then he shook his head

in admiration. "Exactly what *he* always says. Dr. Atkins is a genius. He has made an unbelieveable genetic-diodic match. Nephew, you are exactly what I ordered."

"Thank you, Uncle." I wished I could say the same for him.

"I like the lifeless way you stared from the throne. I like, too, that when we are together I have someone I can talk with, take into my confidence, someone who gives me completely, unquestioning loyalty. It is a lonely life I lead now, Nephew. I have things to do that are very difficult, and which only I can do."

"What things, Uncle?" I asked, trying to sound casual, though my heart was beating hard.

"Tomorrow perhaps we can talk about it. You've had enough input for one day. Now I'm going to lock you into your room. Some well-meaning citizen might want to try to heal you—" he laughed—"and we couldn't have that, could we?"

"No, Uncle."

He patted me on the head. "I am very pleased with your programming, Nephew."

I bowed my head. "Thank you, Uncle. I hope I continue to please you."

"Oh, you will. You are a very superior Atkins robot. Good night, Nephew."

"Good night, Uncle."

He closed the door behind him and locked it. Moments later I heard the council door close. Well, I had to figure a way to get out of this room, get something to eat, and search for signs of the real King Paul.

My window looked down on an inner courtyard. Somewhere down there, on the ground floor, the palace kitchen had to be located.

The castle walls were rough but not rough enough to grab onto and let myself down. I wasn't a human fly.

The window ledges were wider than one would find on ordinary houses. If I was careful, I could possibly work my way down from one ledge to another. It would be tricky. Back home I was a good tree climber, but window ledges aren't tree branches. Still, I had no choice.

I waited till it got darker and the castle settled down for the night.

My room was on the fourth and top floor. Overhead I saw a spaceship flying by. When it got very dark, perhaps I'd be able to see the reflected light of the Atkins rocketship orbiting.

It would be something to look out for.

I waited a while longer, and then when I was sure no one was around in the courtyard, I opened the window. The ledge below was about six feet down. Not a hard jump, but if I lost my balance I'd fall into the courtyard. Better find some rope and ease myself down.

I looked around the bedroom. Of course there was no rope. But there were two sashes on the ends of an old-fashioned curtain rod. Tie the two sashes together, anchor one end to something heavy in the room, and it would be a snap.

I got up on the windowsill and tried to pull a sash off. It was too firmly attached. I needed a knife. One problem was leading to another.

Of course there was no knife in the room. Nothing sharp. Nothing except the bed, the table, and the wheelchair throne. And nothing on the table except the stupid empty striped juice flask from this morning's fast-disappearing breakfast.

Now what? What do I do? What would Danny do? Danny . . . Danny . . . where are you right now? I need your help. Come on, Danny, give me some ESP, give me some of your diode smarts. How do I get a sash down from a curtain rod? All there is in this room is a bed, a table, a wheelchair, and a flask.

I sat and willed and concentrated and thought, and then—faint at first, then louder and clearer— I heard computer beeps. The wonderful life-giving, life-saving Danny One Jameson computer beeps.

And then I heard his voice speaking inside my head:

> It's a dangerous task
> But the only way is:
> Break the flask.

Still teaching me poetry! But the message was clear, and I was surprised I hadn't thought of it.

Thanks, Danny, I thought.

I grabbed the flask and took it into the bathroom. There, against the edge of the toilet, I broke it. Carefully, I picked up one large piece of broken glass, climbed onto the windowsill and sawed off each sash. Now I had two equal lengths of strong sash.

I knotted them together. A square knot. Left over right, right over left. Next I had to anchor one end of the sash to something heavy. The table was too light; it wouldn't hold. The wheelchair was heavy enough, but it would move on its wheels. It had to be the bed. I examined the bed frame. It was made of green stone. Heavy, all right. I knotted one end of the sash to one stone leg and threw the other end out the window.

Unfortunately there was only about three feet of sash to drop down. I had to move the bed closer to the window. Easier said than done. What made the bed a good anchor also made it impossible to budge.

So close and yet so far.

Danny, I thought, Danny . . . I closed my eyes. Help me. What do I anchor the rope to?

The beeps came back in a couple of seconds. And his voice sounded inside my head:

> Sleeper awake!
> The wheelchair brake!

Of course.

I laughed. And the poetry lesson went on. Thank you, Danny, I thought. Wherever you are.

I rolled the wheelchair over to the window and set the brake. This should do it. The chair was heavy and also braced now against the window. I knotted one end of the sash to a wheel and tested it by pulling as hard as I could. The wheelchair throne didn't move.

I tossed the remainder of the sash out the window. It dropped down till it just about touched the ledge below.

I climbed out and let myself down.

9. The Strange Room

Dad says I think okay. I just don't think okay far enough ahead.

I thought of that now as I stood on the window ledge below with no more sash and two more flights to climb down.

Great planning!

Now I had a choice of either climbing into a strange room and then trying to make my way down to the kitchen through the castle stairs, or climbing back into my room and waiting for the duke in the morning and, with luck, another half a hotcake.

I chose the strange room.

I lifted up the window and slid in, headfirst, feeling my way with my hands in the dark. It was like swimming underwater. I was crawling over a windowsill. Luckily, there seemed to be nothing on it for me to knock over.

I kept crawling until I was over the edge of the

sill and one of my hands touched the floor.

Slowly, concentrating on being quiet, I let myself down and stood up. So far, so good. If anyone was sleeping here, I hadn't disturbed him or her.

Now the trick was to find a door that led to the corridor. To find a door in the dark you have to find a wall and follow it till you meet either another wall or a door. If it's a door, you have to hope it's not a closet door. I started off to the right and found the wall. Then I walked along the wall, my right hand touching it in front of me, an antenna feeling for obstructions.

Smack! I hit an obstruction all right. Though it wasn't my hand that met it. It was my knee. My left knee hit something very hard. My knee hurt. I held my breath and waited for someone in that room to wake up and ask: "Who's there?" But no one did. And, come to think of it, I hadn't even heard sounds of anyone breathing in the room. Maybe I'd had the luck to hit on an empty room. Castles have got to be filled with empty rooms. I mean, who can fill up a castle?

I knelt down to feel what it was my knee had struck. It was stone, smooth stone, and very big. And above the stone I felt . . . a mattress. It was a bed. A stone bed. Just like the one upstairs.

I had to get around it. I followed it to the left, feeling my way along its edge, touching the cover on the bed from second to second, feeling its soft plastic fabric, touching it lightly when my fingers quite unexpectedly touched somehing different.

It felt like a foot. Oh God, it was a foot. I froze. I waited. Still no noise. No reaction. No twitch even. Whoever that foot belonged to was sleeping very deeply. I still could not hear the sound of anyone breathing.

I'd have given anything for a flashlight, or even an old-fashioned, strike-it-yourself match.

I touched the foot again gently. It felt strange— stiff, thin, and cold.

A shudder went through my body. No, I thought. It couldn't be. I backed away from the bed. A desire to flee the room swept over me. But Danny wouldn't have run, and I wasn't going to either. I forced myself to stay there.

I had to see what was on that bed. I had to find a light button. It was probably along a wall next to the outside door. I had to find it and turn it on. It could be wrong what I was thinking, but if it wasn't I had to report it back to Dr. Atkins.

As I backed away from the bed, my head struck something hanging down from the ceiling. It felt like an electronic fuse light. Which meant a pulsar button was on one side. I felt around for the button and found it.

My finger hesitated. Did I really want to see what

I thought was on the bed? Would Danny push the light button if he were me? No, Danny wouldn't be here in the first place. I closed my eyes and concentrated on the room and what I thought was on the bed. Danny, I thought, what do I do now? Should I push the button?

The computer beeps sounded inside my head. His voice answered me:

> You've gone this far
> You've got to go farther
> The worst you will see
> Is a royal murder.

The worst? Isn't that bad enough? All right, Danny, I'll push it.

I took a deep breath and pushed the pulsar light button.

A red light began to glow, dimly at first, and then it got brighter and brighter. I steeled myself and turned and looked at the bed.

I gasped. It was what I expected. A waxen, stiff corpse lay on the bed staring up at me with empty eyes. It had been a boy. My age. With freckles. Sixteen on the right cheek and twenty-one on the left. It looked just like me. I looked just like it.

My knees began to shake. My stomach rose up inside me. I had to get out of here right now. I had to get back to Earth. I knew everything now.

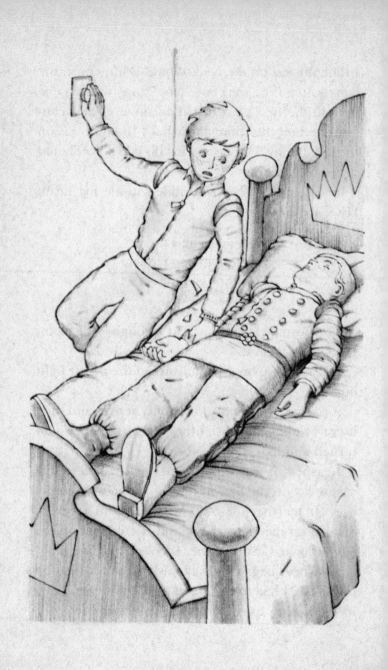

My whole body shook uncontrollably. I reached up to push the pulsar button again and turn off the light. I lost my balance. I had to put one hand onto the bed in order not to fall on the floor.

My hand hit the bed. It also hit Paul's body. One of his arms. My hand went through the arm with a sickening, shredding crackle.

Oh my God . . .

I stared down at the arm. It had a gaping hole in it. Then I touched the shoulder, the chest, the other arm. His skin, his flesh . . . all was soft and crackly, like papier mâché. In fact, it was just that: a dressed up papier-mâché body.

I just stood there not knowing what to think or do. Outside in the corridor I heard the sounds of movement. Soldiers marching. And then voices.

"All's well, Your Grace," a soldier said.

"Excellent," said the duke. "I'm going to turn in now myself. Good night, Corporal."

"Good night, Your Grace."

I had to get out of here fast. But first, I needed to cover my tracks or, better still, the dummy's arm. The last thing I wanted was for the duke to find a gaping hole and start investigating.

I pulled a shirtsleeve down over the hole in the arm. Then I pulled the sleeve on the other arm down to match it. It's amazing how calm you can be when everything in you is telling you to run, jump, fly out of here.

I pushed the pulsar light button and walked quickly to the window, climbed back onto the ledge, closed the window behind me, hauled myself up to my bedroom, and climbed in. I untied the sashes and tossed them under the bed and got back in my wheelchair throne. And there I sat, my chest heaving. Having made it back safely, my calm finally deserted me. I was thoroughly scared and I was thoroughly confused.

If Danny and Fred were up there orbiting, it was time for them to come down and get me out of this mess!

10. Robot Versus Robot

Although I didn't know it then (and it's probably a good thing for me that I didn't), Danny and Fred weren't orbiting Janus at all.

Danny told me later that he and Fred had fought in the rocketship when the duke threatened to blow it up if they didn't leave.

Fred immediately switched on the blastoff controls and Danny just as quickly switched them off. "We can't leave Jack here," he said.

"My first duty is to this ship," Fred said, and turned the controls back on.

"My duty is to save Jack," Danny said, and reached again for the controls.

Fred knocked him away from the console and the rocketship took off. Danny ran for the air locks. He was going to jump out.

"You'll destruct," Fred shouted at him. "We're

up too high. And you won't save Jack by self-destructing."

"Then go back down," Danny screamed.

"No," Fred said. "As soon as we're out of Janus air control I'll radio Dr. Atkins for instructions."

And that's what Fred did. They got Dr. Atkins and told him what had happened. Dr. Atkins hesitated only a second. He ordered them to return to Earth at full speed.

"What about Jack?" Danny asked, feeling miserable.

"Jack's smart," said Dr. Atkins, "and we'll return to help him. You two can't do it by yourselves. You're missing something."

Danny didn't know what Dr. Atkins was talking about. All he knew was that the whole trip back to Earth was the worst time of his existence. Every transistor, every diode, every activator and capacitor, every wire and silicon chip inside him was tingling with anxiety. Fred felt sorry for him.

"I know exactly how you feel, Danny One. I almost lost a spaceship once in Delta system."

"I don't care about your spaceships," Danny said. "You can always build another spaceship. Jack's a human, and you can't build humans like spaceships. I'm supposed to look after him, help him with his schoolwork . . . everything. Oh, it's all gone wrong."

After that, Danny wouldn't talk to Fred. He sat in a corner of the ship, his eyes closed, and worried about me. And that, he told me later, was when we made the ESP contact from Janus, when he heard me asking for help and he helped me . . . with everything.

Knowing I was still alive made the trip a little easier.

Dr. Atkins was waiting for them on the landing pad of the factory. He had a small package in his hand. He ordered the ship refueled and joined them inside.

"We're returning immediately," he told Fred and Danny. "I'm going back with you."

Dr. Atkins looked grim. He kept a tight grip on the small package, holding it in an upright position. Danny had an idea what was in the package. He just hoped that I was still alive for Dr. Atkins to use it.

11. Breakfast Before Breakout

My second morning on Janus was a repeat of my first—with one exception. Tina brought twice as much food on the tray—and, it seemed to me, her smile was twice as mocking.

Once again the duke told her to take it into my bedroom where he would feed me later. Later, I thought, I would probably be dead from hunger.

Once again the large council chamber filled with people—soldiers, civilians, musicians, servants, lawyers—and the endless civil disputes started up again and were settled by the duke, who collected fees from everyone.

I hardly heard a word. I was beginning to feel faint. I didn't care about anything now. Not the mystery of the papier-mâché Paul in the room below. Not the mystery of the real Paul. Not the whereabouts of Danny or Fred. I knew that if I didn't get something to eat soon, I would starve to death on my golden wheelchair throne.

I closed my eyes. Danny, I thought, I don't care if it's in poetry, think into me and tell me what to do. How do I get at that food in my bedroom?

I sat there and concentrated, and seconds later I heard the sounds of his computer beeping into my head and then his voice.

> Your stomach is large
> You've become a weak reed
> Tell the duke it's a charge
> To your battery you need.

Thanks, Danny, thanks.

I tried to catch the duke's eyes. But he was busy collecting money. The sergeant of the guard saw me looking at the duke. He spoke to him, and the duke came over to me, masking his irritation at this interruption with a phony smile.

"What is it, Nephew?" he whispered, bending down, shielding me from the people so they couldn't see my lips move.

"I need a battery charge, Uncle."

It was a lot like saying you had to go to the bathroom . . . at an inconvenient time. His face twisted with annoyance.

"Couldn't you have given yourself a charge during the night?"

"I didn't need it then," I said lamely.

"All right. I'll take you to your room."

"Thank you, Uncle. I can do it on auto-charge."

"You'll have to," he whispered angrily, "I'm very busy today. I've even canceled the rest of this council session. I have business to do, and you'll be alone till two P.M., when I'll return to take you to meet your adoring public. The servant girl will remove your breakfast tray."

For some reason he wasn't afraid of the servant girl, Tina, seeing me privately.

He wheeled me into my room, explaining to people that I needed to nap before my strenuous afternoon when, on the royal balcony, I would be presented to a huge mass of people come to see me.

Everyone looked pityingly at me as he wheeled me by.

As soon as he was gone and the door shut, I grabbed three hotcakes at once, finished the flask of juice in one gulp, ate a square banana, and was starting in on one of the octagonal apples when there was a quiet knock on the door. I hesitated but said nothing, as ordered.

"It's Tina, Your Majesty," said the servant girl. "I've come to collect your breakfast tray."

And without waiting for a "come in," she entered

and closed the door behind her.

"That," she said softly, looking at the half-empty tray on the table, "is a great waste of food. You should not have done that." Quickly she began slipping what was left of the food into the pockets of her apron. Just as she had done yesterday.

"Why are you doing that?" I said.

It seemed perfectly natural to talk to her. And it seemed perfectly natural to her that I should.

"It's none of your business," she said.

I blinked. I couldn't believe she'd said that.

"Sit down, Tina," I ordered. I had to get to the bottom of this.

"I will not sit down," she said, and picking up the empty tray and the empty flask, she poked her nose into the bathroom. "So," she said, "you broke a flask getting rid of the food. Well, I'll clean up later on."

"I order you to sit down," I said.

She looked at me and smiled. "And who do you think you are to order me to do anything?"

My heart began to pound. But I had to go through with the masquerade.

"I am King Paul IV of Janus," I said.

"Is that right?" She laughed mockingly. And then she put her head down till her nose was just inches from mine. "Well, I'll tell you exactly who you are.

You're a robot impostor, and a very stupid one at that. Throwing food away just because you're incapable of eating. I warn you right now. Don't you ever do that again!"

And with that, she turned on her heel and left the room, locking the door behind her.

So the duke wasn't acting alone. He had the help of this pretty but treacherous servant girl.

I had to get out of here quickly. With the council session canceled, the duke off on his mysterious business, now was the time to escape, stowaway on a spaceship leaving Janus. The young king was probably dead.

My job was to stay alive.

I looked down at the inner courtyard. Last night I'd tried to escape going downward, why didn't I try to escape upward today? Get up on the roof and see if there wasn't a way down from there.

I looked up from the window. The parapet of the roof was only a foot or two above the top of my window. If I could grab hold of it and pull myself up . . . Back home in school I was known as a good chinner. Not as good as Danny with all his steel levers and wires, but for a human I was okay.

The courtyard was empty. I started to climb out and then stopped and ducked back into the room. I peered from behind the curtain. Tina had emerged from a room in the palace and was crossing the courtyard, hurrying. I noticed that her apron pockets were bulging. She went into a door on the other side of the courtyard.

Well, the mystery of where she was taking the food would have to wait. My job now was to get out of here.

I climbed onto the ledge and turned slowly so that now I was facing the window. I reached up and got a good grip on the sharp edge of the parapet. Then slowly I pulled myself up and up and up, straining, but doing it until my elbows were level with the parapet edge. Then slowly I wriggled my body over the edge and dropped down, headfirst, onto the roof.

"Boiler," a voice nearby said. "Did you hear something fall?"

I froze.

"Yes," a second voice said.

There were people up on the roof. How dumb of me. I hadn't even considered the possibility that palace soldiers would be stationed on the roof.

It looked as though I'd gone from the frying pan into the fire.

12. Fun in a Funnel

"Don't you think we ought to take a look and see what made that noise, Boiler?" the first voice asked.

"No," said Boiler, "it's none of our business. If some more trash dropped from orbit and made a hole in the roof, our job is to funnel the trash and fix the hole. Not inquire into the noise."

Maybe they weren't soldiers . . .

"Suppose it wasn't trash, Boiler," the first voice said. "Suppose it was a bird that made the hole?"

"Then our job would be to fix the hole and eat the bird."

I almost laughed out loud. In relief. They were workmen, cleaning up the roof of the palace. And from the look of the roof, it could use cleaning. There was lots of trash on it—old boxes, clothes, papers, rotten leaves, rusty machine parts . . .

I peered around an old box. I saw them then. Two middle-aged men who were slowly picking up pieces of trash and putting them into what looked like an enclosed conveyor belt. They wore helmets, and I could understand why. The trash they were picking up fell from the sky, from Janus's trash orbit.

"Boiler," said the first man, "why doesn't anything good ever fall on us?"

"Because," Boiler said, "nothing good's in orbit."

"Boiler, you're very smart."

"Thank you," Boiler said. "I'm throwing the switch."

Boiler touched something on the pipe, and there was a rushing noise. The trash was being blown across the roof inside the pipe. But to what end I couldn't see.

It was clear I couldn't stay here. I had to put some distance between those two odd workmen and me. So I crawled away from my spot, being careful to keep air vents, old boxes, a satellite dish between me and them.

I crawled crab style to the other side of the roof. And there I saw what was happening to the trash on the palace roof.

The pipe blew it into a large funnel, the stem of which ran down alongside the castle wall and emptied into a solar garbage truck parked below.

I wasn't on the courtside of the palace now, but

overlooking the front—a huge main square with all of Janus City stretched out beyond it.

There were the gates I must have come through the other night. And soldiers patrolling the gates.

It must be in this square that the citizens of Janus would be gathering this afternoon to take a look at their invalid young king. Well, I hoped to be a long way from here. Where exactly I didn't know, but somewhere where I could board the Atkins rocketship.

Where that would be I hadn't the slightest idea. First things first. I had to get off this roof and disappear in the city beyond the royal square.

My eye was caught by movement below. A door opened in the palace and a familiar figure emerged. It was Tina. She had crossed the inner courtyard and was now leaving the castle proper. Her apron pockets, I saw, were still bulging.

She walked quickly across the square. I decided she was probably delivering food to a poor family in the city.

Suddenly she stopped. She turned toward the solar garbage truck. She was talking to someone inside it. The driver opened a door and gestured to her. He was offering her a ride.

And that was when I saw how I could get out of here. My escape route was staring me in the face. It was ready made. A quick trip down a funnel and a ride through guarded gates inside the trash in the back of the truck. It was beautiful if smelly.

All I had to do was jump into the funnel. The stem or tube part looked wide enough for my body.

Keeping my head below the parapet, I crawled over to the funnel in order to study what was the best way to get inside it.

The trash blown from the pipe shot a gap of a few feet before it disappeared down the funnel and stem. It was only a matter of timing for me. I had to jump into the funnel between loads of trash shooting the gap.

What I now had to do was time the intervals between trash deliveries.

Some kitchen scraps shot the gap from the pipe into the funnel.

"One transistor, two transistor, three transistor, four—"

An old broom and some rags shot through.

"One transistor, two transistor, three transistor, four—"

Old tools and papers.

"One transistor, two transistor, three transistor, four—"

About four seconds between shot loads. I could do it if I moved quickly.

I waited. A load of broken bricks shot the gap. Thank God I hadn't jumped before them!

Now, I thought. Now!

I leaped up onto the parapet and dived head-first into the yawning funnel.

It was wide, it was inviting, it was smooth. It was also pitch black as down and down I went in a dark, tumbling spiral, swoosh and swish and whoosh and wish, and wash and whee, skidding from side to

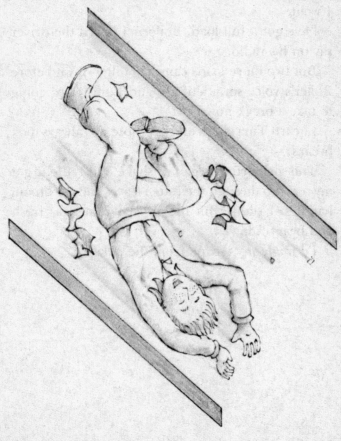

side, rolling over and over, yelling in the dark, screaming as hard as I could and not knowing I was doing it till my echo came after me and I tumbled into the light and garbage of the solar garbage truck.

I was laughing hysterically. I started to sit up, then I got hit by a load of rotten leaves and down I went.

"I've got a full load, Boiler," I heard the driver say on his radio.

But two more loads came shooting down before Boiler's voice sounded. He and Louis were going to take a break now.

I heard Tina laugh and say those two always took breaks.

The solar truck began to shake and rattle. I got my nose up through the rotten leaves and the broom handles. I stank. But the air above me was fresh and beautiful.

I'd made my escape from the palace.

13. The Invisible Hand

We rattled past the guards at the main gate without any trouble. Soon we were driving through the streets of Janus City.

I lay beneath a thin layer of trash and on top of some nice soft spongy garbage. I was quite comfortable. From where I lay I could see the top floors of buildings. I figured to hop off the truck from the rear end when the driver let Tina off at the front end.

Right now I could hear the two of them arguing. Tina was saying it was stupid to put trash in orbit when in time some of it came back down.

The truck driver laughed. "Where else you going to put it, Miss Tina? Besides, I *like* putting trash in orbit over and over. It's a steady job for me."

Of course, I thought. This load of trash is being taken to a spaceport to be shot into orbit. All I have to do is stay put.

"Now," the truck driver went on, "I think you got yourself a nice steady job for a youngster. Easy, too. Here you are off on a picnic in the middle of the morning."

"I happen to be working," Tina protested.

"With all those hotcakes tucked in your pockets and headed for Pond Eight?" The truck driver laughed good-naturedly. "That's only the best fishing pond on Janus. None of us can get near the place, and that's where the palace people hold their picnics. Oh, I get around. I hear a few things, you know. Still now, I don't know as I envy you being a palace worker. Being around that poor lad must be depressing. Can't walk, can't hardly talk, invalid all his life. I hear that before the duke got him his latest operation the poor devil just lay in bed all day long hardly breathing."

Good Lord, I thought. That explains the papiermâché body. It was a temporary body the duke needed till he had an Atkins robot to sit in for Paul. Which meant, I thought, with a sinking heart, that the real Paul was dead.

"I guess living in a wheelchair is an improvement for him, isn't it, Miss Tina?"

Tina was silent. The truck driver laughed. "Won't talk, huh? Well, that's what happens to palace people. They got too many secrets to keep. Still, it's a nice day for fishing . . ."

The truck rattled on, and so did the driver. Soon the tops of buildings gave way to tops of trees. Odd-looking trees, but we went by them too fast for me to identify them.

After a while Tina interrupted one of the driver's monologs to tell him she would get out here.

"I always wondered where Pond Eight was," the driver said.

"Wonder on," Tina snapped. "I'm going to do some walking yet."

"Well," the driver said good-naturedly, "don't eat too much and leave some fish for us common folk in case we ever find Pond Eight."

The truck stopped, and I heard Tina get off. I was tempted to see where she headed, where the great Pond Eight was, but she might be watching the truck, making sure it moved off. So I lay there and thought fishermen everywhere had a hard time sharing good fishing spots.

The truck picked up speed. It hit some bumps, but the garbage cushioned most of them. After about ten minutes the truck stopped. I buried myself a little deeper in the garbage. A voice from above called down:

"Another load from the palace?"

"That's right," the driver said.

"Pass on in. Let's hope this load stays up a long time."

The other voice obviously belonged to a control-tower guard at, I hoped, a spaceport. I lay very still. It's motion that catches the eye more than anything else. At this point, I was sure I looked more like garbage than a human or a robot.

We picked up speed again, this time driving over a smooth surface. My guess was that it was a landing pad. After a while we slowed down, stopped, backed up, and then stopped. It seemed to me the driver had maneuvered the truck into a very specific spot.

Now was the time to get out. I pushed aside my trash cover just in time to see the sky turn from blue to black. A dark cloud was descending fast on the truck, blocking out everything, fastening onto the sides of the truck.

It came with its own built-in thunder, too. The sounds of a deep motor and, like a tornado on Earth, it began sucking things up.

I felt myself being lifted up along with the rags and leaves and garbage and broken bricks and broom handles. Lifted up in the palm of a huge invisible hand, lifted up and up and up—and going upward faster and faster.

I screamed. I realized what it was. The trash and I were being sucked up into a huge vacuum and then into a large hose, spinning, tumbling over and over, my face covered with trash, my body covered with rotten leaves, up and up we went all inter-

mingled and then we tumbled over an invisible hill of air and rolled down the other side, landing together in a heap inside a shelter, a structure, a house . . .

I pushed the trash off my face and looked around. The sides of the shelter were curved, aerodynamic. I saw air locks. An inner air lock and an outer. I knew where I'd landed—in the cargo bay of a rocketship. There was a sign on one curving bulkhead. It said:

JANUS TRASH DISPOSAL SERVICE
The Garbage Orbit People

I laughed. You've been in some odd places in your life, Jack Jameson, but maybe this is the oddest.

Then I stopped laughing. Another load of trash came tumbling down from the vacuum hose and into the cargo bay. And more after that. Suddenly I realized that I could die very easily in this cargo bay. The trash was mounting fast around my knees.

I waded through it to the sides of the ship and pounded with my fists on those sides.

"Help," I shouted. "Help! Help! Help!"

14. The Big Spill

All I was doing was making myself weak. No one could possibly hear me pounding on the door, the noise of the vacuum motors was so loud. I had to do something else and do it quickly. The trash was up to my hips, and mounting.

Danny, I thought, give me the diode smarts. Just one more time. I don't care if it's another poem. Danny, Danny, help me. I silently described to Danny the fix I was in.

Sure enough, in just a few seconds the computer began to beep inside my head. And then I heard his voice saying:

> A ship's a ship
> Though its cargo's trash
> Open the air locks
> And make a dash.

That simple. But when you're in a panic, you don't see things simply or clearly.

By now the trash was almost up to my shoulders and was over the air lock handles. I pushed and shoved and cleared a path to the inner air lock handle. I turned it and pulled. It was hard work. The trash pressed against it, and every second more was being dumped in from the overhead hatch. I pulled with the desperation of a drowning man.

Slowly the inner air lock opened. As it did, however, trash flowed around the edge and slapped up against the outer air lock.

I moved fast, and began to turn that handle. It was in the middle of turning it that I realized something funny was happening inside the rocketship. Something had changed. The noise had stopped. The vacuum motors had been turned off. The ship was silent. No more trash was coming in. I looked up. The overhead hatch was being sealed.

That could only mean one thing—the ship was getting ready to blast off. I had to get out and get out fast. And get out without being seen.

The trash pressed against me and against the sides of the ship. It was my only chance.

I yanked as hard as I could on the outer air lock handle. It flew open. And everything that was inside the ship, including me, flew out—sticks, mops, bricks, leaves, garbage, trash. . . . I tumbled out with a protective screen of debris, and as I fell I could hear shouts:

"There's a spill. A big spill!"

"The air lock's opened!"

"Stop the flight!"

"Call the pilot!"

I hit the ground on top of a bag of old rags and was immediately dumped on by a pail of meat slops and old pillow feathers. And still the stuff poured out.

I couldn't see anyone, which may have meant they couldn't see me either. I started crawling through the trash, away from the ship. I had just aborted a rocketship blastoff and trashed a spaceport. I wouldn't be too popular here.

Through the falling trash, I saw figures running to the ship. I got to my feet and ran, too. But I ran away from the ship.

A man came up to me. "You all right?" he asked.

My face was covered with feathers and food slops.

"Yes," I said. "Close the air lock," I shouted.

He ran toward the ship, and I ran till I was off the pad, away from the shouts of the spaceport technicians. No one was watching me. They were watching the trash spill out of the ship.

I could see trees and bushes lining the edge of the spaceport. I made a dash for them. There was a fence there. I climbed it and jumped down from the top and ran for the safety of the trees. Once among them, I threw myself down on the ground.

My chest was heaving. I wiped the garbage off my face and looked back.

The ship was surrounded by people and machines that were scooping up the garbage. The technicians were blaming each other.

I got up and plunged deeper into the forest.

15. Forest Fortress

Running through a thick forest is hard at any time. But when you're scared, don't know where you're going, and the forest is on another planet, it's twice as hard.

Just to start with, the trees were different. They were sort of all alike, symmetrical, as if they were built rather than planted. And they were shaped like no trees on Earth.

The first trees I saw had five-sided fruit hanging from them. Pentagonal peaches, they looked like.

As I ran I grabbed a pentagonal peach and almost pulled my arm out of my socket. It was practically welded on. Not ripe or not real. I kept on running.

The next batch of trees not only looked weird, they *acted* weird. They were all tall and skinny and had vines twisting around their trunks. As I ran by, a vine reached out and snapped its teeth at me.

I stopped and stared. Those vines were really snakes growing out of the tree. Mechanical snakes with sharp teeth and nasty darting tongues. Good God, what kind of forest was this?

I ran the other way and spotted, just in time, a cloud of darts coming at me. I ducked. The darts passed over my head. When I raised my head, another volley of darts flew at me.

I lay down. One of the darts landed near me. I picked it up. It was really a large steel thorn. Slowly I peeked to see where this fusillade of thorns was coming from.

Ahead of me was a thick hedge, like a wall, filled with the thorns. My guess was that the hedge was really an electronic bush that had sensors and activators in it because the moment I rose to my feet, it shot another volley of thorns at me.

No one back home would believe this. I picked up one of the thorns and put it in my pocket. Then I crawled backward out of there. I backed and backed until I could go no farther. I turned, and my head was stuck. Stuck in a noose.

A bunch of ropes had descended from a tree and were tightening their strands around me. I pulled the noose off and ran away from a stand of rope trees. Those trees had twine, string, and ropes growing from the ends of their branches—

thickish-looking cobwebs, and deadly to unsus-
pecting people.

This was no natural forest. Thorns that shot at
you, vines that bit you, ropes that tried to strangle
you. This forest had been fabricated for a purpose.
To protect something. What?

Perhaps if I climbed a "safe" tree I could get a
look around.

The only safe tree seemed to be the pentagonal
peach tree. Like all fruit trees, it shouldn't be hard
to climb. Its branches were close to the ground,
and I was a good tree climber. At least back home
I was.

I shinnied up a few feet to the first branch and
then grabbed hold of that welded pentagonal peach
and pulled myself up. With the welded peaches, it
was the easiest tree in the world to climb. I wondered what kind of protection this tree afforded.
Probably it was to lure people in.

I climbed as high as I could until I could see past
the snake trees and beyond the thorn hedge. What
I saw now were rows and rows of bamboo thickets
with bamboo stakes coming out of the ground like
soldiers' spears. And beyond the bamboo . . .

I caught my breath. It was beautiful. Two little
ponds almost touching each other, forming a figure
eight. Pond Eight?

It had to be.

On the slender isthmus between the ponds there was a hut. It looked habitable.

There had to be a way to that pond that didn't get me messed up with thorns and sharp bamboo stakes. I guessed it was time for some diode smarts again. And so, clinging to a couple of pentagonal peaches, I willed Danny into my head. I described the scene silently and asked for help.

Sure enough it came, and again in poetry.

> Rivers feed oceans
> Streams feed lakes
> Creeks feed ponds
> Build a raft of stakes.

I let go of the peaches and slid down the tree.

16.   Raft Ride

About a hundred feet off to the left, hidden by a screen of bamboo and some rope trees, I found the creek. I also found a lot of bamboo stakes lying on the ground. Soon I had about thirty of them. To make a proper raft I'd need to lash them together.

With what?

I looked around.

> Raft of hope
> Tree of rope

I thought, making a bit of a rhyme on my own. Well, I'd get even with the rope trees by cutting some of their ropes down.

With what?

I felt in my pocket.

You've got a knife
And it's not worn
It's very sharp
And called a thorn.

A pretty feeble rhyme, I guess, but again, I made it on my own. I fetched my souvenir thorn out of my pocket and worked its sharp edge across the rope. I cut one strand, then another, and another, until I had one rope down. Then I went to work on the other ropes. Before too long I had enough to lash my bamboo stakes together.

I found a long stake that would act as a combination rudder and pole, and now I was all set. My destination was that hut on the isthmus between the two small ponds that made up Pond Eight. I had the sense that someone was living there. Someone who could help me get to a communication center, which in turn might help me get off this planet.

I cast off, poling off the embankment, and almost fell into the water. I found that the safest way to steer was to lie flat on my belly and pole from a prone position. The raft skittered sideways, hit a rock in the middle of the creek, and then another rock. It took me a while to get the feel of it, its balance. But after a while the raft and I became buddies and we began to float freely down the creek.

I got pretty good at spotting rocks and poling away from them and using the creek banks to get us back into midstream.

This was fun. For the first time since I'd been here I forgot I was a million miles from home and passing under a couple of false identities. I like water. To fish in, swim in, raft over.

Making that little raft was one of the best things I'd ever done in my life. Danny would have been proud of me. So would Mom and Dad.

I was very tempted to lie on my back and forget about Pond Eight and going home. My raft and I floated past bamboo thickets, past thorn hedges that shot their thorns in over my head, past snake trees with vicious little snake heads that lashed their tongues at me in frustration, past other kinds of strange, vicious-looking bushes and trees.

The creek wound in and out and then speeded up as it came around a bend. There was white water now where it rushed along. The raft began to skitter.

Ahead I saw a brown metal barrier, blocking the stream.

A dam.

The ponds were manmade, too.

I poled vigorously over to the bank on my right, jumped off onto the shore and pulled my raft up behind me. Then I crawled through some high grass, up a little hill, and looked down.

I was at Pond Eight, and it was as beautiful close up as it had been far away.

17.   The Kingnapping

The hut I'd seen from the treetop was placed exactly where the two ponds looped together to form the figure eight. Someone was fishing on the far pond, but the hut blocked my view of him or her. Every few seconds, though, I saw a fishing line flicker out, lie still on the surface, and then get pulled back.

Whoever was dry fly fishing could do it very well.

The pond was quiet and pretty. A long way from palaces and laser guns and cold-blooded dukes. I could stay at a place like this a long, long time, I thought. But it was time to get moving again. To find out where a communication center was located.

I had started to crawl toward the pond when a door in the hut opened and Tina came out. She was carrying the hotcakes, apples, and bananas on a small tray. She walked around the hut and disappeared.

I crawled forward, angling off to my left so I could see around the hut. I heard Tina's voice, but I couldn't hear what she said or what the person fishing replied.

I kept crawling, keeping a screen of tall grass between me and them. I could see Tina now; she was holding out a hotcake to someone, and now that someone came into view and took it.

"Someone" was a boy. A boy my age. A boy with brown hair and freckles. Only this time he was *not* made of papier mâché. He was, thank God, flesh and blood!

A lot of thoughts raced through my head. One, Paul was alive; two, he was a prisoner here; three, Tina worked for the duke by feeding the prisoner; four, the duke was taking a big chance letting him live now that a robot likeness of his was on the throne; five, what should I do now?

Not knowing what to do, I just lay there in the grass and watched them. Tina and Paul were arguing about something. It seemed to me Paul was telling her to go away, that he wanted to fish. And she was insisting that he stop and eat. He took the hotcakes off the tray and ate them, then he started fly-casting again.

Tina took the tray back into the house.

I still wasn't sure what my move should be. If Tina weren't around, I'd have no qualms about going up to Paul and telling him who I was and what I was supposed to be. But if Tina was working for the duke . . .

Well, I couldn't lie here all day. I tried to think what Danny would do. He'd probably go to Paul and tell him everything. Maybe Tina wouldn't be looking out the window. Now was the time. Get going.

I had started to get up when I heard a swooshing noise in the sky. I ducked back down. A space cruiser shot over the pond, made a tight circle, and then landed right near Paul.

Tina stuck her head out the window. You could see she was surprised, too.

Paul didn't seem surprised. He went on fishing.

A ramp extended from the cruiser, and down the ramp came the duke followed by six soldiers

who were led by the sergeant of the guard from the palace.

"What are you doing here, Uncle?" I heard Paul say to the duke.

The duke didn't answer him. He turned to the sergeant of the guard. "There is the imposter," he said. "You can see he's not sick. Arrest him."

"Are you crazy, Uncle?" Paul said.

The sergeant of the guard raised his sword. "Put him under arrest," he ordered his soldiers.

"What are you doing, Sergeant?" Paul demanded. "Don't you know me? Have you gone out of your mind, too?"

The soldiers, carrying laser rifles, ran up to Paul and twisted his arms roughly behind his back.

"Let me go," Paul shouted. "This is a mistake," he yelled. "I'm your king," he begged.

But it was no use. They pushed him along up the ramp and into the air cruiser. The duke followed them up the ramp. Seconds later the air cruiser rose and shot off.

Not thirty seconds had elapsed from the time I first heard the swooshing noise in the sky. A king-napping had occurred—quickly and efficiently.

Now Tina came out of the hut. She was crying. That baffled me completely. Why would she cry if she were working for the duke?

She stood there a second, undecided what to do,

and then, still weeping, she ran down a path away from the pond.

There was no point in going to the hut now. And this was no time for me to try to leave Janus. This was a time—if there was any time left—to try to save Paul.

I hurried in the direction that Tina had gone.

18. People Flood

I had to move fast to keep Tina in sight. She ran frantically down one path after another and finally ended up in front of a laser fence camouflaged with leaves and branches. This was probably the front entrance to Pond Eight. I must have come in the back way.

She unlocked the gate and hurried on through without bothering to lock it behind her. I guess it wasn't important anymore to keep the gate locked since the prisoner was gone.

I waited till she was out of sight. Then I slipped through the unlocked gate. When next I caught sight of her, she was running toward a main road. A road that, to my astonishment, was jammed with people—old people and young, fat ones, thin ones, men, women, children, farmers, miners, clerks. It looked like everyone on the planet Janus was in motion, and all going the same direction. Some were

driving solar cars, others were flying in airlift scooters. Most were walking.

There was a holiday spirit in the air. Some people held balloons that had faces painted on them. Correct that—a closer look told me there was only one face painted on the balloons. Mine. I mean, King Paul's.

Groups of students came by, arm in arm, dancing, and singing gaily:

> Paul is back
> Paul is back

Clickity-clack
King Paul is back.

Hawkers stood by the side of the road selling flags, whistles, candy bars, and big floppy hats that had the words WELCOME HOME, KING PAUL stitched in big letters around the brim.

I suddenly remembered what this had to be all about. They must be on their way to the palace, to the royal square, to see Paul appear on the balcony on his wheelchair throne.

What time was that to be? Two P.M., the duke had said. He would return to the royal bedroom to fetch me at two P.M.

I glanced at someone's watch. It was one-fifteen. Forty-five minutes to get back to Janus City, to get into the palace, to get into the royal bedroom, to get back on the wheelchair throne.

I had to do it. Because a plan had formed itself in my mind. I had to join this flood of people. But even that would be tricky. I looked an awful lot like the face on all the balloons.

As I stood there some kids my age came by singing the "Paul is back" song. If I could slip unnoticed into any group, it would be this one.

I waited till they were alongside, and then, singing as loudly as I could, I ran into the road and sang and danced along with them.

We swung by a hawker of hats. "I'll take one," I called out. "How much?"

"Free today; tomorrow you pay," he laughed.

I pulled the brim of the hat down over my face, but not before a girl dancing next to me smiled at me and said: "You look familiar."

I tried to keep my voice casual. "People tell me I look a lot like King Paul."

"Of course. Won't it be wonderful to see him again? Even if he can't walk or talk?"

"It will be wonderful," I agreed, and sang out as loudly as I could:

> Paul is back
> Paul is back
> Clickity-clack
> King Paul is back.

19.   Accessing a Palace

There was no problem getting into the royal square. All the gates were wide open. It was a national holiday declared by the duke in honor of Paul's return. No school for anyone. The duke was a hero with everyone.

The real problem would be getting back into the palace. With thousands of people milling about in the square, waiting for Paul to appear, every door was being guarded by a soldier with a laser rifle.

I glanced at someone's watch. It was almost two o'clock. I had to move fast. But the soldiers guarding the doors looked grim and immovable.

I closed my eyes and thought hard about the wild scene I was part of and pleaded with Danny in rhyme:

> Danny One
> Have a heart
> Will me some
> Diodes smart.

I guess my ESPing in rhyme really moved him. His computer beeps came back right away. I heard his voice:

> Break some balloons
> Make some noise
> Soldiers will come
> Like curious boys.

The balloons were everywhere. If I could pop four, five, six of them quickly, it would sound like gun fire.

What would I pop them with? I felt in my pocket, and there it was still: the thorn that I'd cut the ropes from the rope trees with.

But I had to move fast. Suppose someone saw me, grabbed me—worse, shot at me.

Standing there, I must have looked worried. One of the girls I'd marched to town with asked me if I felt all right.

"I . . . uh . . . feel fine," I said. "I . . . uh . . . have to see someone."

I walked away from my group as fast as I could.

"I wonder what's bothering him," I heard someone say.

And someone else answered: "It's always a problem when you look like someone famous."

In front of me was a group of adults holding King Paul balloons. One was held by an old lady. Another by a man. I could start with them.

I had the thorn in my hand. No one was looking at me. They were all looking toward the royal balcony. It was five minutes still before Paul was supposed to appear. I just prayed the duke hadn't arrived at the royal bedroom to find it empty.

Here goes nothing.

I walked casually past the old lady's balloon. And then quickly I pricked it.

Pop!

I hit the balloon held by the man.

Pop!

I swerved and knocked off two balloons held by a skinny kid.

Pop! Pop!

And then two balloons held by two kids my age. (I didn't discriminate.)

Pop! Pop!

By this time the popping of the balloons had attracted attention. People started yelling, jumping up to see what was going on, pointing this way.

I hit one more balloon on my way toward the palace doors. The soldier guarding the door nearest me hesitated. I ducked behind a fat man and stuck my thorn into his balloon.

It exploded.

That did it. The soldier, his laser rifle extended in front of him, ran toward us.

I ran around the fat man and for the unguarded palace door.

20.   Home Sweet Throne

"Ja-nus, Ja-nus," the sergeant of the guard called out.

"Ja-nus, Ja-nus," the squad of six soldiers chanted back as they marched up the stairs from the palace basement. The same soldiers that had arrested Paul at Pond Eight.

Crouching in an alcove on the ground floor of the palace, I watched the soldiers make a right turn and continue on up the stone steps, chanting: "Ja-nus, Ja-nus."

I waited a few more seconds before moving, and it was a lucky thing I did. I wasn't the only one hiding on the ground floor of the palace. A figure detached itself from an alcove down the hall and ran down the stairs, the same stairs the soldiers had just come up.

For a moment I was tempted to follow Tina once more. But there wasn't time. It had to be very close

to two o'clock. I'd be in terrible danger if the duke didn't find me on my throne.

I pulled my hat down and ran up the stairs. Outside I could hear the noise of the huge crowd waiting in the square. Above me I could hear the soldiers' chant floating down the stairwell: "Ja-nus, Ja-nus."

As interplanetary chants went, it wasn't bad. Better than marching to "Earth, Earth."

When I got to the fourth floor, I saw the soldiers marching toward a set of double doors way at the end. The doors swung open for them, and the roar of the crowd increased. The doors shut and the crowd noise died down.

Which meant those doors led to the royal balcony. But which door led to the council chamber and to my wheelchair throne?

> If you want to play Paul
> You better try them all.

That wasn't Danny talking inside me. That was me.

All right, I'd try them all. But should I walk into the corridor like a human or a robot?

> You came as a robot
> You're not home free
> It's safest to walk
> Stiff-in-the-knee.

My brains were really clicking along in rhyme. If ever I got back to Earth and Miss Mortenson's class, it wouldn't be a wasted trip.

I walked stiff-in-the-knee out into the corridor and began opening doors one after another. A closet door, another bedroom door, doors into servants' quarters, doors into weapons closets. There were at least twenty more doors to open.

Whirr . . . whirr . . . whirr . . .

I ducked into an alcove. A door I hadn't opened, opened across the hall. It was an elevator door. Tina came out. She ran down the hall, opened a door, and ran in.

I ran to it, too, figuring I'd have time to duck into another alcove before she came out again. But I didn't. I only had time to walk stiff-in-the-knee again as she caught me.

"You," she said with contempt. "You better get back on your wheelchair, robot, because soon you're really going to need it."

"Tina, wait a second. I have something to tell you. I'm not—" But she didn't wait to hear what I had to tell her. She brushed by me and ran past the elevator to the stairs.

She was angry and she was frightened at the same time.

I went into the great domed council chamber just as the clock struck two. In the bedroom my wheelchair throne was where I'd left it. I sat down in it and closed my eyes, trying to relax.

It was hard to believe I'd only been gone three or four hours from this room. I felt as though I'd lived three or four lifetimes.

I hoped now the duke hadn't come by earlier and seen the wheelchair empty. Well, I'd soon find out.

I could hear the duke coming before I saw him. There was the usual royal folderol of trumpets and the sounds of boots in the corridor, and then the duke came into the royal council chamber and into the bedroom.

He smiled when he saw me, which told me I'd got back in time.

He closed the door behind him and sat down on the bed.

"Ah, Nephew, what a strenuous day it has been so far. And I haven't yet accomplished what I hoped to accomplish."

He looked at his watch. "We must go to the royal balcony now, Nephew."

"What was it you hoped to accomplish, Uncle?"

The duke rose and patted me on the shoulder. "For your sake and mine, Nephew, I had hoped to be able to do away with an impostor once I got him back to the palace dungeon. But there wasn't enough time. And I can't trust anyone to do it but me—"

he looked down at me and smiled again, that thin, cold, cruel smile I was getting to know so well—"and perhaps you. Yes, when this foolish presentation on the balcony is over, you and I will kill this impostor. You will enjoy that, won't you, Nephew?"

"Yes, Uncle."

He chuckled. "Once he's dead, all our problems are over. And now we must go to the balcony. Remember, Nephew, not a word do you say, not a finger do you lift. I'll be standing next to you at all times. If something should go wrong with your programming, I will remove you instantly and break into your computer myself. Is that clear?"

"Yes, Uncle. Nothing will go wrong."

He patted me on the head and wheeled me out of the room.

21. "Long Live King Paul!"

When the double doors slid open, it was like the ocean rolling in. Only it was noise instead of water.

"Long live King Paul!" came a shout from a hundred thousand throats.

You could *feel* the noise.

"Long live King Paul!"

There they were, as far as the eye could see, waving their flags and balloons.

The duke set the brake on my wheelchair. Then he started to talk into the microphone. But they wouldn't let him.

"Long live King Paul," they kept chanting.

And then the chant changed and a new chant rose from the square. It seemed to come mostly from the kids, who shouted:

"Paul . . . Paul . . . Paul . . . Paul . . ."

Over and over. As if by shouting that one word at me over and over somehow I would be made

well again and my muscles would move and my tongue would speak and I would rise up from my wheelchair.

"Paul . . . Paul . . . Paul . . . Paul . . ."

The chant was begging me. Thousands and thousands of young faces looking up at me. And thousands and thousands of my own face bouncing in the air reaching as high as the balcony.

I searched the crowd for the group of kids I'd marched with, but they were impossible to spot. I did spot the squad of soldiers from Pond Eight and the basement, led by the gray-haired sergeant. Holding his ceremonial sword in front of him, he and they were clearing a path through the crowd.

They marched to the foot of stone steps that led up to the royal balcony from the square. The sergeant positioned two soldiers at the bottom step and then a soldier on every tenth or so step going up. And then he positioned himself on the top step where the stairway met the balcony.

Once there, he put his sword in its scabbard and looked sternly out at the crowd that was still shouting:

"Paul . . . Paul . . . Paul . . . Paul . . ."

The balcony shook under the noise.

"How they love you, dear Nephew," said the duke with a tender smile on his face.

"Paul . . . Paul . . . Paul . . . Paul . . ."

Beaming, he again took the microphone in hand. His first words fooled me completely. He was clever.

"Long live King Paul!" he shouted into the microphone, and his voice echoed from loudspeakers placed all about the square.

"Paul . . . Paul . . . Paul . . . Paul . . ." they shouted back.

"And he will live a long time!" the duke shouted into the microphone. And that quieted them down a bit.

"But alas," he said, and hesitated, and now there was a silence. Oh, he was a very clever speaker. "Alas, his life will be different than the one we expected and hoped for."

And now the square was so silent you could have heard a transistor drop.

"However," he said softly into the microphone, "through the miracles of medical science our young king's life has been saved . . ."

Overhead I heard the faint sounds of a rocket-ship.

". . . but, alas, medical science is unable to come up with a way to make King Paul walk again, or talk well again—"

"That's not true," came a cry from the crowd.

Everyone looked to see who had yelled that.

"The real Paul can walk and the real Paul can talk," the person shouted.

I peered at the crowd. People were pointing at . . . Tina. She was standing below us and causing a great stir. People yelled for her to be quiet.

"I won't be quiet," she said, "that's not the real Paul up there."

Things were getting out of control. Beyond the square I saw the rocketship coming down for a landing. Probably at the Janus City Spaceport. No one except me paid any attention to it.

The duke turned calmly to the sergeant of the guard. "Take the poor girl inside. She's obviously lost her mind."

"People, listen to me! The real King Paul is in the palace dungeon," Tina cried out.

The sergeant looked sad about what he had to do now. He made a motion with his sword. The two soldiers on the bottom step moved toward Tina. But Tina surprised them. Instead of running away, she ran toward them, and then past them and up the stone steps.

She *has* gone mad, I thought.

She was up on the balcony now. She ran to the microphone and lowered it to her height. The duke made an angry motion at the sergeant of the guard.

"Listen to me, everyone," Tina pleaded. "The

real king is awaiting death right now. He's—"

The sergeant of the guard took her arm and gently pulled her away from the microphone. "Tina," he said, "the one in the dungeon is an impostor."

"No," Tina said, "the impostor is right here in that wheelchair, sergeant. He's in a wheelchair because he's a robot, not a human being. When he walks, he walks stiff-in-the-knee. He's made of wires. I'll prove it to you."

Before he could stop her, Tina grabbed the sergeant's sword, pulling it out of its scabbard and ran with it toward me.

"I'll show you its wires," she shouted.

A gasp went up from the crowd.

"Someone stop her," the duke shouted.

But no one did, and I noticed he wasn't offering to put his own body between me and the sword.

I waited till the last moment, hoping against hope that someone would stop Tina. She was running with the sword pointed right at my heart.

When she was only ten feet away and coming on fast, I jumped out of the wheelchair and ran. I ran to the farthest end of the balcony. And I didn't run stiff-in-the-knee either.

At the end of the balcony there was nowhere else to go. But I needn't have worried. Tina just stood there, sword in hand, staring at me with an incredulous expression.

The duke was as amazed as she. And the huge crowd was stunned, too. The great awed silence was finally broken by a little boy who cried:

"He's cured. King Paul is cured!"

And with that a wave of joy swept the square. People wept, embraced, fell on their knees . . .

And then slowly the chant started up again: "Paul . . . Paul . . . Paul . . . Paul . . ."

But this time it was a chant of triumph, not begging.

"No," Tina screamed, "he's not the king. He may be a human being, but he's not the king. The real king is in the dungeon."

Her shouts were lost in the noise of the crowd.

"Speak! Speak! Let King Paul speak!" they began to shout.

If I could walk, then I could talk. But the last thing I wanted to do now was speak. I looked at the duke. He was staring at me curiously. Who was I anyway, I could see him thinking.

I realized then this might be my only chance to save Paul.

I advanced on the microphone.

22. Now We Are Three

I'm not a very good public speaker. I don't know any kid twelve years old who is. Miss Mortenson says it's important that we learn to speak in front of others. (In case we run for President, I guess.)

Miss Mortenson has even composed a little rhyme to help us not be nervous when we get up in front of the class.

> Be clear
> Sincere
> Show cheer
> Not fear.

Right now, as I stared out at the huge mass of people filling the square as far as my eye could see, I felt a lot of fear. My heart was pounding; my throat felt dry.

I could see people hanging onto the palace gates to get a better view of me.

Be clear.

I cleared my throat. A dry sound echoed around the square. And people cheered. That made me feel a little better. If they cheered me when I cleared my throat, they might cheer anything. Including the news that I wasn't who they thought I was.

How to begin to tell them the truth? Where should I start?

And then it seemed to me that instead of quieting down, the cheering grew louder. And it seemed to be coming from far off, even beyond the gates. I could hear a faint chant getting louder and louder:

> King Paul is back
> King Paul is back
> Clickity-clack
> King Paul is back.

I'd thought that chant was done with already. But it had obviously started again and was getting stronger. It was coming from a procession of people who had emerged from a narrow street and were marching toward the square.

They chanted and pushed their way through the gates and elbowed their way into the crowd, a moving stream entering a large body of water.

I saw they were carrying someone on their shoulders. The crowd began to part for this procession. People stood on tiptoe to see what was happening. They had stopped looking up at me.

As the small procession got closer, I could make out who was being carried to the palace in triumph. It was a boy my age with brown hair and freckles.

Walking alongside him was another familiar figure—a tall, white-haired man in a long laboratory coat. And next to him was a wide-shouldered robot with a big mustache. He wore a pilot's uniform.

I felt relieved. Not even Tina saying to the sergeant: "That's not him either, I tell you he's in the dungeon . . ." worried me. The fact was I was no longer alone on Janus. Danny was back, and with a new set of freckles. And Fred was with him. And Dr. Atkins was here, too.

I laughed with relief as the procession, chanting, shouting, made its way up the stone steps. I saw Tina take something from the sergeant's outstretched hand. It was a key. She ran into the palace.

I looked at the duke. He hadn't seen that little incident. He was watching the procession come onto the balcony. He looked more puzzled than worried about the arrival of a second king of Janus.

The people carrying Danny wore spaceport uniforms. They let him down gently and bowed to him, and then they saw me, and they bowed to me, too, a little confused now.

Danny and I threw our arms around each other.

"Are you all right, Jack?" he whispered.

"Fine. Where've you been? What's going on?"

"I'll explain later. We just landed. The people at the Janus City Spaceport think I'm King Paul."

"The people here think *I'm* King Paul."

There was a buzz of unease in the square. No one knew what was going on. A little girl in the crowd called out: "Papa, why are there two King Pauls up there?"

The duke went into action. Ignoring me and Danny, he spoke into the microphone.

"Good people of Janus," he said. "Both of these boys are impostors. Sergeant, arrest them both. Take them to the dungeon. There we'll learn what they've done with the real King Paul."

"They've done nothing to me, Uncle," said a voice behind us. "It was you who planned to kill me."

Everyone on the balcony turned. There in the doorway stood a third Paul, though this one was not dressed like a king. He was dirty and disheveled, but his eyes were flashing regally and angrily. Next to him stood Tina, looking flushed but triumphant.

"Papa, now there are three of them," the little girl cried out.

And now other people shouted from the crowd.

"No more tricks!"

"We want the real king!"

"Which of them is Paul?"

The duke, who I thought should have been scared stiff by now, smiled coolly at the crowd. He has ice in his veins, I thought.

He spoke calmly into the microphone. "None of them is the real king, my good people. They are all impostors. And all will be punished for their crime. Sergeant, arrest them all!"

"One moment," said someone who had not spoken till now. I had been wondering when Dr. Atkins would take over. I'd never known him not to take charge of anything.

Holding the small, mysterious package in his hands, Dr. Atkins strode up to the microphone.

"Citizens of Janus," Dr. Atkins said, his voice echoing around the square. "My name is Leopold Atkins, and I am director of the Atkins Robot Factory on Earth."

The duke frowned, but still he didn't look alarmed. My guess was that he had still another trick up his sleeve.

"As the number-one robotics engineer in the universe," Dr. Atkins went on, "I hold a responsibility for your present confusion. Only one of these three is the real king, and I intend to clear this confusion up for you right now."

Dr. Atkins opened the package and took out a jar of the thick whitish liquid that had messed things up in the first place for me and Danny.

Dr. Atkins turned to Danny. "You first," he ordered.

He dabbed freckle paint remover onto Danny's cheeks and then wiped it off. Almost all of Danny's freckles disappeared.

There were oohs and ahs from the crowd as word spread from those near the balcony to those far away.

"Now you," Dr. Atkins said to me as though he had never laid eyes on me before. He dabbed the freckle paint remover onto my face and wiped it off. From the oohs and ahs I could tell that most of my freckles had disappeared, too.

Finally, Dr. Atkins turned to Paul. "Come here, young man," he ordered.

Only Leopold Atkins would order a king around like that. But Paul went to him, and Dr. Atkins applied the freckle paint remover to Paul's face and all the freckles stayed there. Where they belonged.

"Here is your true and right king!" Dr. Atkins raised Paul's hand.

"Long live King Paul," the crowd shouted.

Paul turned to the sergeant. "Arrest my uncle on a charge of high treason."

The sergeant of the guard moved to the duke's side, but the duke calmly waved him aside.

"You cannot have me arrested, Nephew . . ." The microphone picked up his words and carried them to all corners of the square. "The fact is, this whole thing was your idea. Tell everyone the truth, Nephew. It was you who planned this whole masquerade."

What an amazing villain, I thought. To save his skin, he tells the most incredible lie in public.

I waited for Paul to laugh in his face.

But Paul was silent. Finally, he spoke into the microphone. "Good people," he began—and hesitated. He took a deep breath and started again. "Good people of Janus . . . what my uncle says . . . is true. It *was* my idea to put a robot king on a wheelchair throne in my place."

It was the world turned upside down. Everyone stared at him. Including me and Dr. Atkins.

And the silence in the square was ominous now.

The people had been fooled often enough. Now all tricks were over, all cards had been played. Now the people wanted the truth.

Paul spoke again.

23. Kingly Confession

"I want to apologize to all my subjects," he said quietly, though his words carried to every corner of the square. "I thought it would be a harmless trick I'd be playing. You see, I did ask my uncle to order a robot likeness of me. I was very bored sitting there day after day in the council chamber . . ."

I could understand that, all right.

". . . I wanted to live as other boys my age lived. I wanted to go fishing, swimming, play games. But my uncle said the king's business could not be conducted without the presence of the king."

He spoke without embarrassment, though he spoke with deep regret.

"Then one day I saw on a Read/Screen that a robot factory on the planet Earth had made a robot buddy for an Earth boy. That gave me an idea. I talked my uncle into ordering a robot likeness of me who could sit in for me in the council chamber.

"And I mean 'sit,' because if my double walked everyone would know right away it was a robot." Paul stopped and looked at me and Danny. "Which of you was to be my robot 'sit-in'?"

"Me," said Danny, and he walked stiff-in-the-knee around in a circle.

Paul nodded. "You can see why we would have to find a reason that he couldn't walk. So we started a rumor that I had a terrible disease. A disease that would leave me in a wheelchair all the time.

"But I couldn't wait for the robot to arrive. I wanted to go off fishing on Pond Eight right away. So I had a paper dummy of me made who would lie in bed and be sick all the time. When the robot arrived, we would destroy the dummy. And when the time came for me to really be king, when I was thirteen, I'd make a miraculous recovery from my wheelchair. And we would destroy the robot."

Danny winced. Dr. Atkins looked grim. Paul looked apologetic.

"My good people," he went on, "the whole thing was bad and foolish. I made you all worry about me. The only person who knew the truth besides my uncle was my servant Tina. She was to bring me the food the robot couldn't eat, and thus nothing would be missing from the kitchen food accounts . . ."

It really was a good plan, I thought. Everything was accounted for.

Paul shook his head sadly. "I also agreed with my uncle that my robot buddy should be programmed for complete obedience to him so it would sit through all those boring council sessions."

And now Paul's face changed from being apologetic to looking angry.

"What I didn't know, good people of Janus, was that my uncle would take advantage of my plan and try to send me on a vacation that would never end. He was planning to kill me and then rule forever in my name, using the robot and my so-called disease. And this would have happened except that, as Tina just told me, the royal robot buddy turned out to be a human being. And—" Paul looked at me—"I don't know yet how that happened."

"I do," I said.

I joined him at the microphone and told the citizens of Janus all that had happened, starting with the beeps in the night, my wanting to go with Danny to the robot factory to get out of my poetry assignment, Dr. Atkins's suspicions, how I became a human mirror for Danny, the bump in space that washed off Danny's freckles, the switch that had me, a human being, pretending to be a robot pretending to be a human being.

The huge crowd was very quiet. I told them about my escape from the palace by way of the funnel, my near escape from being sent into a trash orbit, fighting my way through the electronic forest outside of Pond Eight, coming back to the palace, popping the balloons, and finding my way back to the wheelchair throne.

"The rest you know," I said, "except that I didn't know that Danny One, *my* robot buddy, would be back with a new set of freckles."

"I never wanted to go to Janus in the first place," Danny confessed to the crowd. "I don't like troubles, but I had to return to look after Jack. It was Dr. Atkins's idea to give me a new set of freckles. He thought it might come in handy to play the king."

Dr. Atkins permitted himself a smile. "It certainly got us through the crowd and up here."

And then the smile left his face. He turned to Paul. "It's always dangerous when kings, especially youthful ones, decide to play tricks. To be a king is to be a privileged person. But to be a privileged person means also giving up a certain amount of freedom. Your trick was dangerous to your kingdom and dangerous to yourself."

Paul nodded. "I know that now. Thanks to Jack and Danny, though, it came out all right. The question now is, Dr. Atkins, what do I do about my uncle? He was my adviser; he ruled in my name; and he was going to kill me."

Paul turned to look at his uncle, but there was no uncle there. In the excitement of Paul's confession, the duke had slipped away.

"I'll find him, Your Majesty," the sergeant said.

"No, Sergeant," said Paul, "let him go. All of Janus knows him and knows what he tried to do. That will be his punishment. After all, I am partly to blame, too. My uncle is an ambitious man, and I put something in front of him that he could not resist."

Dr. Atkins nodded approvingly. "That was a very kingly thing to say, Your Majesty." He turned to the crowd. "I think I do not err when I say to one and all that King Paul, young as he is, is truly a king now, tested by adversity and tempered by experience. I suggest to you that he should rule from now on in his own name."

A great roar of approval went up.

"Thank you, Dr. Atkins," Paul said quietly. "I think I can rule now. I've learned a lot. First, I want to promote the sergeant to captain of the guard. It takes a brave and intelligent soldier to listen to a servant girl rather than a duke."

"Thank you, Your Majesty," the new captain of the guard said.

"As for you, Tina," Paul went on, "you'll no more be my servant. I hereby appoint you head of the royal household. You were loyal and you were brave and I'll need your counsel more than ever."

Tina's eyes were moist. You could see how much she loved and admired Paul.

He was only a boy our age, but he was also every inch a king, even in his dirty clothes.

Paul turned to me and Danny. "As for you two, I don't know how to thank you for the risks you took."

"I didn't take any risks," Danny said. "I don't like risks."

"You came back with freckles," Paul said with a smile. "And around here that is taking a risk. Jack," he said, turning to me, "your wish is my command."

"Well," I said, "I'd like to come back to Janus some day and fish Pond Eight."

Paul laughed. "Agreed. I officially declare that Jack Jameson has fishing rights forever on any pond on Janus, but especially on Pond Eight."

"I'll be back," I promised him.

Danny sighed. "And I guess I'll be back to see that he doesn't fall in."

Everyone laughed.

24. The Last Big Bump in Space

After that the musicians played and all the balloons in the square were released so that Paul's face floated high in the skies of Janus.

Danny and I shook hands with everyone. Tina was a little embarrassed shaking hands with me. "And to think I wanted to cut you open and show your wires to everyone."

"Hey, before that you tried to starve me to death."

We both laughed at that.

I asked Paul if I could show Danny, Dr. Atkins, and Fred the council chamber where I'd been king for a little while.

"Of course," Paul said. "I'll go with you. I want to make sure my uncle isn't hiding in the palace."

We found no sign of the wicked duke, but we

did find the old crate I'd been delivered in. I showed Dr. Atkins the tiny air holes Danny had made for me.

"Ruined a perfectly good crate," Dr. Atkins grumped. "We'll have to throw it out."

"You can drop it off in the trash orbit on your way back," Paul said.

"No problem," said Fred.

Paul ordered a soldier to carry the crate out to a solar car and take it to the rocketship. I guess Janus soldiers are pretty weak because the guy needed help, and in the end it took two of them to carry out the crate.

After that we said our goodbyes, and I invited Paul to fish the pond behind our house on Earth.

"It may not be as good fishing as Pond Eight," I said, "but you won't have to fight your way through a manmade forest to get to it."

Paul laughed. "I'll come if you promise you won't paint freckles on your face again."

"You don't ever have to worry about that," I assured him.

Paul saw us off at the spaceport. The crate had already been taken on board. Dr. Atkins lectured Paul once more about not fooling people. He also told him that one secret to wielding power was to be able to put up with boredom.

Paul grinned at us. "I can put up with it already," he said.

Danny and I laughed. It was a good thing Dr. Atkins had a bit of a sense of humor, though he didn't have an awful lot.

We closed the air locks and waved goodbye from the window. The ramp came up; the motors went on; the landing legs retracted and slowly we rose.

Soon the spaceport got small, the city shrank, the ponds in the countryside looked like drops of water, and by then we were way up in the Janus atmosphere and beginning to hit some air bumps. We went through the Janus gravity curtain without any trouble, and ahead of us I could see the Janus trash orbit. A set of old bed springs went sailing by as I watched.

Danny said it was time for me to get started on my poetry assignment. "You'll be in school by the day after tomorrow, and Miss Mortenson is going to want to hear the poem you wrote."

"Okay, I'll get to work on it."

I'd avoided my poetry assignment long enough.

"This is probably as good a spot as any to dump the crate," Fred called back. "We're passing through a major trash orbit."

He was holding the controls tightly, trying to avoid hitting trash as well as pockets of air that escaped from the Janus atmosphere.

Dr. Atkins sat alongside him, keeping an eye on the things.

"Do you two need help with that crate?" he called back to us.

"No, sir," I said. "I carried it by myself a while back. Open the air locks, Danny, and I'll shove it out."

Danny opened the inner air lock and was going to open the outer lock, but I couldn't budge the crate, no less pick it up.

"Something's got to be inside it," I said.

I slid the lid off and my heart almost stopped.

The Duke of Janus was lying there inside and holding a laser pistol pointed right at my heart.

"I was hoping to reach your planet undetected, Mr. Jameson," he said calmly. "However, you've changed my plan."

Keeping the pistol pointed at me, he got out of the crate.

"Since it is not my intention to go into a trash orbit around Janus for the rest of my life, and since I must get rid of you before we reach Earth, perhaps it's best if you took my place in the crate."

Behind the duke, next to the outer air lock, Danny closed his eyes. He was concentrating, willing into me . . .

When I didn't move, the duke said: "You will either climb into that crate or die right now." His

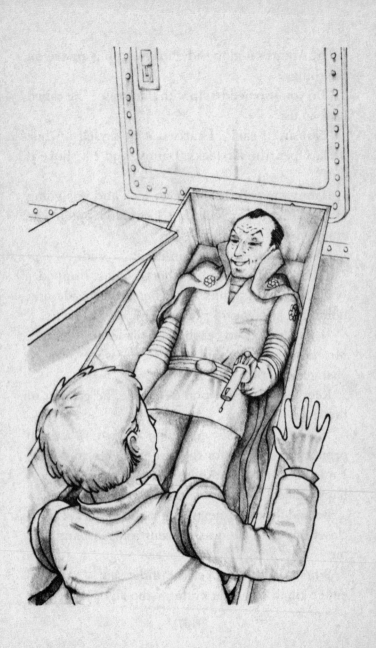

finger tightened on the trigger.

Here it comes, I thought. And it did. In rhyme:

> You be me
> I'll be you
> We'll pull the old
> Switcheroo.

"You think I'm Jack Jameson, don't you?" I said. "Well, I'm not. I'm his robot buddy, Danny One." I walked stiff-in-the-knee in a small circle, just as Danny had done on the royal balcony. "We fooled another one, Jack."

"We sure did, Danny," Danny said from behind the duke.

The duke, distracted, turned. I jumped for him. But I never got there. At that moment, despite Fred One's best efforts, our ship hit a big pocket of escaped Janus air.

We were all jolted sideways; the crate slid toward the outer air lock.

Danny, with computer speed, opened the air lock just as the crate slammed into the duke from behind, and out they both went, crate and duke, through the open air lock.

We slammed the air locks closed and ran to the nearest porthole. Our last view of the duke was him floating away inside the air pocket (he was really quite lucky when you think about it), trying to push

off a bundle of old rags with one hand and some old solar car parts with the other. The crate was chasing him in orbit.

"Sorry about that bump," Fred called back to us.

And Dr. Atkins added, irritatedly: "I'm going to register a complaint with King Paul about all these Janus bumps."

"Don't do that," we both shouted at once, "we love Janus bumps."

And for once in his life Dr. Atkins was properly astonished.

25. "Has Anyone Seen the Duke of Janus?"

All good things come to an end—even adventures.

Two days later I was back in school. Miss Mortenson said to me (just as Danny predicted she would): "Well, Jack, did you work on a poem while you were gone?"

"Yes, ma'am."

I had worked on one all the way home. Dr. Atkins and Danny and Fred all liked it. But Miss Mortenson would be a lot tougher audience. And so would the class.

"What's the title of your poem, Jack?"

" 'Has Anyone Seen the Duke of Janus?' " (Which was pretty close to the poem I never finished—"Has Anyone Seen the Trout in the Pond?" I guess poets have certain rhythms that belong to them and to no others.)

"Very good," she said. "Come to the front of the class and read it to us."

I got up and went to the front of the room. For once I wasn't nervous. Talking to thousands of people in a palace square is a pretty good preparation for reading a poem to your sixth-grade classmates.

I took a deep breath and read in a loud and clear voice:

> Has anyone seen the Duke of Janus?
> Who tried to commit a crime so heinous?
>
> He's up in the sky where he belongs
> And as he orbits he sings this song:
>
> Alas, alack
> If not for Jack

I'd be the king
Of everything.

Instead I fly
Around the sky
Trying not to crash
Into other trash.

The class burst into applause. Miss Mortenson applauded, too.

"Jack," she said, "that was excellent. It's clear to me that you worked on your poetry during your latest adventure."

"I did, ma'am. It got me out of a lot of troubles on Janus."

"Wonderful. However, I'm sure the class would like to know—I know *I* would like to know—what the poem is all about. Who is the Duke of Janus? What was the terrible crime he tried to commit? How does he fly around the sky with trash? Tell us about it, Jack."

"Yes," the class echoed, "tell us about it."

"Well," I said, "it all started with beeps in the night. Three of them to be exact:

beep beep beep . . ."

Which is, I think, where you came in.

ALFRED SLOTE lives in Ann Arbor, Michigan. He is the author of many novels for young people. His novel JAKE was an ABC Afterschool Special called *Ragtag Champs*. Among his most recent books are RABBIT EARS and CLONE CATCHER. THE TROUBLE ON JANUS is the fourth book about Jack Jameson and Danny One. The others are MY ROBOT BUDDY, C.O.L.A.R., and OMEGA STATION.

JAMES WATTS grew up in San Francisco and went to school at the University of California at Berkeley and the California College of Arts and Crafts. In 1983 he received a Society of Children's Book Writers grant. His artwork for THE TROUBLE ON JANUS is his first published work.